THE SECRET OF THE FORTY STEPS

THE FOURTH CHRONICLE OF A LADY DETECTIVE

K.B. OWEN

MISTERIO PRESS

The Secret of the Forty Steps
The Fourth Chronicle of a Lady Detective
Copyright © 2020 Kathleen Belin Owen

Published in the United States of America

~

Cover design by Melinda VanLone, BookCoverCorner.com

~

ISBN-13: 978-1-947287-17-4

CHAPTER 1

Newport, Rhode Island
Friday, June 17, 1887

"*It* should only take a minute," I said to my friend Cassie, as we stepped out of the summer sunshine of the town square and into the cool dimness of the First National Bank of Newport.

She tucked a dark strand of hair back into place beneath her best summer straw as she sank onto a vestibule bench. "One can only hope." Her voice rasped with fatigue.

I couldn't blame her. Our journey from Chicago to Newport had been riddled with railway delays and transfers that had us dozing in uncomfortable bench seats these last two nights and breathing in more coal smoke than I cared to contemplate. Even a simple errand on our way to our final destination, a local cottage owned by Lady Ashton, seemed an intolerable delay.

But I could hardly turn down a request from my employer, William Pinkerton of the Pinkerton Detective Agency, who wanted me to deliver a sealed, confidential document directly into the hands of the bank president once I arrived for my holiday in Newport.

"I'd rather not trust it to the mail," Mr. Pinkerton had said, signing it across the sealed flap and passing it to me.

"I don't suppose you can tell me what it is?"

He shook his head. "Have a nice visit with your family, Mrs. Wynch."

I was so preoccupied with turning my laugh into a cough that I barely registered annoyance at his continued insistence upon using my married name. One family estrangement at a time.

Visit with your family. Is that what it was? I didn't know quite what to call it. My mother's telegram, after nine years of silence, was simultaneously clear and cryptic in its summons:

I URGENTLY REQUIRE YOUR ASSISTANCE IN A PRIVATE MATTER. BRING SUITABLE ATTIRE FOR BRIDGET'S WEDDING ON THE 25TH OF JUNE.

It was just like her to assume I would come. She was counting upon my curiosity overriding all else. She was correct, of course.

After confirming our plans by return telegram and receiving the address, we bought tickets for the next train.

I'd been puzzling over the telegram the entire trip. What private matter? And why would she ask for *my* help? My mother, Mrs. Curtis Hamilton, dominated the social register of New England bluebloods, set society trends, and hosted the most sought-after soirees. The woman was the embodiment of self-sufficiency. For her to make an urgent request of anyone, particularly the disgraced daughter she'd been obliged to explain at every cocktail party, banquet, musicale, and charity ball in the early years of my absence, was completely out of character. She certainly wasn't desperate for me to attend Cousin Bridget's wedding. Such family affairs over the years had come and gone without invitation. That part was a ruse.

At least I had an ally. I looked back over my shoulder at the slightly built, dark-haired Cassie Leigh, gloved hands smoothing her skirts as she sat. It hadn't been difficult to persuade my long-time friend and housemate to come along. The promise of fresh ocean breezes and scenic vistas was sufficient. Fortunately, our underpaid-but-self-sufficient maid back home was able to handle our lodgers in the meantime.

I passed through the inner pair of doors to the First National as a top-hatted gentleman came out the other side. It was the noon hour, so a good many patrons were taking advantage of the lunch break to conduct business here. He tipped his hat politely before moving on.

No one was staffed at the desk area beyond the polished mahogany railing, so I waited my turn in line before moving on to the next teller available.

"A deposit, miss?" he asked politely, tilting his head to peer up at me through his thick spectacles.

"I wish to see Mr. Fisher, if you please. I have something to deliver to him."

"Indeed?" He turned toward a lad sitting on a stool behind him. "Fetch Mr. Fisher."

The boy took off, and the teller waved at me impatiently. "If you would step aside and wait, there are patrons behind you I must attend to."

The teller had just finished with his second customer when a short, stout gentleman, his brown pinstripe vest straining at the buttons, approached and gave a little bow. "How may I be of service, miss?"

I lowered my voice and explained my errand.

His eyes brightened. "Excellent! Come, we'll go to my office. Much more comfortable there. My staff can bring you a cup of tea, Miss—?"

"Hamilton. I appreciate the kindness, but I must be going. I have a friend waiting—"

I broke off as something caught my eye. To my right was a bowler-hatted man of middling age, the second patron who had come up to the teller window after me. He now stood at the counter-high writing table set aside for customers to sign bank drafts and count their bills. The man was rather encumbered, struggling to set down his umbrella, overcoat, a tin from the grocer's, and finally, the bank envelope of bills, no doubt to count them before leaving.

What had attracted my attention, however, was a lean, sandy-haired fellow with a capacious mustache. He was close behind the man, his eyes watchful.

"Miss Hamilton?" Stokes prompted.

"Shhh...look." I inclined my head toward the pair, just as the younger man reached under the other man's elbow, toward the table.

Fisher sucked in a breath. "Stop! Sneak thief!" he thundered, pointing.

Both men froze and gaped at us for the barest of moments before the light-haired fellow took to his heels.

Realizing Mr. Fisher's intervention was limited to pointing and shouting, I gave chase, dodging patrons and passing my startled friend as I sprinted through the vestibule. Out on the sidewalk, I caught a glimpse of the man turning the corner, but by the time I got there he was nowhere in sight. The distant rattle of coach wheels over the sound of my racing heartbeat suggested an accomplice with a waiting vehicle. I swallowed my disappointment as I struggled to catch my breath.

Cassie was standing anxiously just outside the bank when I returned. "What on earth is going on, Pen?"

"I'll tell you in a minute. Can you summon a hackney? I'll be right out."

Back inside the bank, Mr. Fisher was soothing the man in the bowler hat. "Now then, Mr. Tompkins, don't you worry, we'll catch him." Fisher looked at me, and I wordlessly shook my head.

The man—Tompkins—gathered his belongings with shaking hands, his glance darting back to the door as if expecting the man to reappear and accost him once more. He groped for his kerchief and mopped his brow. "Nothing taken, so there's no harm done. I'm just grateful you stopped him, sir."

Fisher puffed out his chest. The vest buttons nearly mutinied in response but held fast in the end. "Not at all, not at all. We stay on our toes, you know. A necessity in our business."

Tompkins tipped his hat and left, with barely a glance my way.

I was just as eager to leave at this point. I pulled out the sealed envelope entrusted to me. "I must be going, sir." I lowered my voice. "This is the document Mr. Pinkerton said you were expecting."

"Ah." He tucked it in his jacket pocket. "Please pass along my thanks." He squinted at me more closely. "Are you sure you don't want to sit and rest a while, my dear? You cannot be accustomed to the exertion of pursuing would-be thieves."

Oh, wouldn't I? I glanced away to conceal my grin and spied a bit of blue beneath the writing table. "It appears your customer has left his tin behind." I was about to suggest that if he hurry he could catch up to Mr. Tompkins, but it was obvious Fisher hadn't hurried a day in his life, and I'd had enough of chasing people for today.

"Well, bless me," he said, crouching with some difficulty to retrieve it, "the poor fellow *was* rather flustered. I'll get it back to Mr. Bennett."

I frowned. "Bennett? You called him Tompkins."

"Tompkins is Mr. Bennett's valet, likely engaged in errands for the household."

"Are we talking about James Gordon Bennett, owner of the *Herald*?" I asked.

"The very same." He puffed his chest once more, at least as

5

far as the buttons would allow. "Keeps his yacht here in Newport. We're privileged to have him doing business with us when he's in town."

During our ride to Lady Ashton's cottage—dubbed The Cedars, according to my mother's follow-up telegram—I told Cassie what happened.

Her eyebrows shot up. "And you say he took all the credit for spotting the sneak thief? The cheek of the man!"

I shrugged. "It happens more often than not. I just wish I'd caught the miscreant."

"Well, you certainly catch your share."

We were quiet for a while, watching idly as we drove along spacious avenues where stately villas of every type—Gothic, Colonial, Queen Anne, shingle-style, and more—sprawled beyond our view.

The bank incident had been a temporary diversion from the worry of seeing my mother after all these years. It returned in force as we pulled up to the circular brick drive of the Ashtons' cottage.

Cottage, of course, was a misnomer. *Mansion* was a better term for the double-winged, three-story structure, with a deep front porch and eaved windows trimmed in ornate scroll-work.

Cassie was quick to sense the shift in my mood. "It could be a positive sign, you know, her sending for you." She gathered her purse and jacket as we came to a stop. "Perhaps she wants to be reconciled."

I rolled my eyes. "Not likely."

But she wanted *something*.

CHAPTER 2

$\mathcal{I}$ knocked briskly upon the oak-paneled door.

"Enter!"

The peremptory voice of Honoria Hamilton, the undisputed matriarch of the Boston branch of the family, had not changed in the years since I'd last heard it. I expelled a breath and let myself in.

The lady turned from the window at my approach, looking me over in a frank appraisal.

Those who meet me for the first time generally assume I come by my height from my father, but in actuality it is my mother who passed along that trait, along with—if I'm to be truthful—a mulish nature and an abiding impatience with the feckless people of this world. Thankfully, I did not inherit my mother's prominent hooked nose which, combined with a pair of piercing gray eyes, can chill one to the marrow.

I returned her look with an appraisal of my own. After all, the last time I'd seen her was just after Frank and I had eloped, when we'd returned to explain ourselves.

She hadn't altered much over the years—a bit thinner, and her hair, as pale blonde as mine, now shot through with conspicuous threads of silver. Her eyes were as sharp and clear as ever.

"Sit down, Penelope." She gestured toward a chair as she settled herself on the divan, arranging her foulard silk into graceful folds. Her eyes flicked over my best mulberry linen walking suit, several years out of fashion but made over to accommodate the more modern cuirass silhouette. "You'll want to freshen up before dinner. Even in Newport, we do dress for the occasion."

As our luggage had arrived ahead of us and I'd not had a chance to unpack, I dearly hoped the wrinkles in my dinner dress would smooth out by then.

"I must say," she went on, "I am surprised you accepted my invitation to attend Bridget's wedding."

It was impossible to miss the fact that she omitted *pleasantly* in characterizing her surprise.

"As fond as I am of Cousin Bridget," I answered bluntly, "I would have declined under ordinary circumstances. But you said you needed my help. What assistance do you require?"

"I would not have required anything from you," she snapped, "but it seems I have little choice. I need someone to make discreet inquiries."

I blinked. "Inquiries? *Me?*"

She impatiently waved a be-ringed hand. "You are one of those lady detectives, are you not? Employed by the Pinkerton Agency?"

It took me a moment to realize my jaw was hanging slack. A most unladylike expression. I shut it. "How did you know?" My voice grew tight until it was nearly a squeak. "Did…Frank tell you?"

"*Humph.*" It wasn't quite a snort—Mother never snorts, it's undignified—perhaps it was more of a sniff. "If *that man* ever had the audacity to write to *me*, the servants know to throw such a missive directly into the fire. No, *that man* did not tell me."

Frank Wynch, my now-estranged husband who had been a Pinkerton longer than I, had been *that man* in Mother's eyes even before we'd married. Papa had first hired him—much against her wishes, I might add—to investigate the theft of a family heirloom. Frank had found the heirloom but made off with the daughter, so to speak, and Mother had steadfastly refused to speak his name aloud since. What she said about him to herself, of course, was another matter entirely.

How had my mother learned about my work for the agency? Back in Chicago, I considered myself safely removed from the world of East Coast high society and wealthy elites, who in winter make their money from steel, coal, railroad, and banking industries, and in summer take their ease in sprawling mansions termed "cottages," congregating in exclusive areas such as Newport, Martha's Vineyard, and the Hamptons.

Cassie and I, on the other hand, lived in quiet obscurity, running a boardinghouse to keep body and soul together. Of course, things weren't so quiet and obscure whenever Mr. Pinkerton decided a lady's touch was needed and assigned me a case—to uncover a department store shoplifter, a fare-skimming streetcar conductor, or a jewel thief plying his trade at a lakeside resort. I found myself smiling at the latter memory. I've met the most interesting people while on a case.

But how she'd discovered it…my mind was a blank. "Well? Are you going to tell me how you found out?"

My mother grimaced. "In the most awkward way imaginable. Lady Ashton came up to me at the spring cotillion, wanting to know if you had actually turned your hand to *detective work*. It seems a senator of her acquaintance—Cullough? Callem—?"

"Cullom," I supplied, my stomach sinking. I could see where this was going.

"Yes, that's it. Well, this senator could not stop singing the praises of a woman named Penelope Hamilton, a lady detective who had saved his niece and her friend from kidnappers. Lady Ashton, naturally, pressed him for more details, and she soon had a description of the lady in question." Her eyes narrowed. "You."

9

Land sakes. So much for living in obscurity. "And how did you respond?"

She scowled. "You cannot possibly believe I would deign to debate the particulars of such an outlandish story? You may rest assured I put Lady Ashton in her place. I maintained that the man had been teasing her, as he had deemed her gullible enough, poor dear, to fall for such a tale. By the time I was done with her, she was no end of contrite at giving it any credence at all."

I smothered a smile. To have been a fly on the wall listening to that particular conversation....

"In fact, she felt so badly about the entire matter that she offered the use of this cottage while they travel abroad this month. Most convenient for us, as it coincides with Bridget's wedding."

"I wondered how you came to be staying here without the Ashtons. But I take it *you* had no difficulty believing I was a private detective?"

She waved a dismissive hand. "As your mother, I am aware of the more, *ahem*, unconventional aspects of your nature."

I let that go. "What did you tell your friends about my whereabouts after I left?" I wasn't sure why I was curious now, when I'd never cared before.

"Simplicity itself. As none of the eligible young men seemed to suit—the '77 season was rather sparse in that regard, save for Leonard Frasier...why you two did not marry is beyond me, but the point is now moot—I explained that you had developed a keenness for the old temple ruins of Siam and decided to make it your life's work."

"Temple ruins?" I echoed. It is a strange phenomenon of upper crust society that personal eccentricity can be forgiven, but a daughter's elopement to a man below her station is only to be pitied—and of course gossiped over, whether it be the intimate salon or the crowded cotillion. "If you were going to be that outlandish, Mother, you might as well have me doing missionary work to convert the Buddhists."

Did I glimpse a faint smile?

"Oh, no one would have believed *that*, dear. However, you've always taken an interest in the most dreary topics and obscure locales, so my version was eminently believable."

A quick knock on the door was followed by the maid bearing a tray laden with a delicate, bone-china tea service. It was Mother's own private set, monogrammed with *HH* in gold leaf.

After the tea was poured and the maid left, I asked, "What sort of inquiry do you wish me to make?"

"It concerns Bridget." She absently stirred the dissolving sugar cube in her cup, not meeting my eye.

The silence stretched between us.

I finally broke the lull. "Ah, Bridget!" I kept my voice casual. "It's hard to imagine her old enough to be marrying. I still recall her as a little girl, scrabbling about for interesting-looking rocks to collect and scraping her knees in the process. Tell me about her now. I'm behind on the news." As I'd learned from Mr. Pinkerton, sometimes it's necessary to overcome a client's reticence by first discussing related subjects, then gradually warming up to the problem at hand. Mother or no—we were virtual strangers to one another these days, anyway—it seemed necessary here, too.

Her eyes took on a faraway look. "Bridget is twenty-three now. A charming young lady—when she exerts herself." She dropped her voice to a mutter that I barely caught. "All too fond of rocks, even still."

"I'd heard about her parents' death," I said. "That's when she came to live with you and Papa, is that right?"

"Nearly seven years ago," she said. "Frankly, I'd despaired of her ever being married, so I was happy to see Reg Collinsworth taking an interest—" Her brow furrowed. "But at this point, I'm not so sure."

At last. I leaned forward. "The problem is with the

husband-to-be?"

Wordlessly, she slipped an envelope out of a book resting on the side table and passed it over.

The envelope was plain but not cheap, the paper being of a thicker weight. The mailing address was printed in unremarkable block lettering. There was no return address, but the cancelation stamp indicated it had been mailed locally in Boston to the Hamilton brownstone in the city. I unfolded the note, also a thicker variety of paper.

BE WARY OF YOUR NIECE MARRYING COLLINSWORTH, OR SHE MAY MEET THE SAME FATE AS HIS FIRST WIFE. ~ A FRIEND.

The block lettering matched the envelope.

"When did you receive this?"

"Last week, shortly before we left for Newport."

I tapped the envelope. "It looks to have come in the regular mail."

"Yes, it accompanied other letters."

"So Collinsworth had a first wife—is he much older than Bridget, then?"

"Not really—he's twenty-eight. But his first marriage was a brief one—it lasted only a year, in fact."

"What happened?"

"His first wife died in an accident."

I didn't like the sound of that. "What sort of accident?"

"I don't know many details. I was told she fell from a seaside path near here, known as the Cliff Walk. The locals say some sections are rather treacherous, particularly in damp weather."

"Oh? Was it raining that day?"

"I have no idea."

"Was there an investigation?"

She shifted impatiently. "I imagine so. Otherwise, he would be in prison instead of inheriting her millions."

I resisted the urge to roll my eyes. "In other words, you know nothing about the investigation into the death of his first wife—what was her name?"

"Eunice Ivey, before she married. You may remember her. She was an avid patron of the arts. We attended some of the musical soirees she hosted at her home in Boston, though that was ages ago."

It was indeed. Most of what I recollected were long stretches of boring conversation, interspersed with a few, bright moments of glorious arias. I frowned. "She was a good bit older."

"By twenty years. It caused quite a stir at the time."

"Does Bridget know about the note?"

"I didn't want to alarm her. It could be pure spite."

That was a possibility, though the circumstances of the first wife's death were disturbing and should be looked into. A young man marrying an older, rich woman, who dies suddenly in an accident...the penny dreadful nearly wrote itself.

"Who would feel spiteful toward Bridget?" I asked.

Mother bit her lip. "I hesitate to name her. I don't wish to malign someone unjustly." Her brow darkened. "It is a sordid business."

"Nevertheless," I said, "we must face it, unpleasant as it is."

"Perhaps you are accustomed to such in your dealings. *I* am not." She abruptly got up and crossed the room, stopping at the window. She kept her back to me as she spoke. "Rebecca Blakely is a possibility."

"And who is she?"

"She's Bridget's best friend and will serve as lady of honor at the wedding."

"And you believe someone so close to Bridget could have sent the note?" I asked incredulously. "Why?"

"Miss Blakely was enamored of Reg. He escorted her to several functions before shifting his attentions to Bridget."

CHAPTER 3

"Ah, there you are!" Cassie called out from the path. I was perched on a flat boulder near the shore, wringing sea water out of my hair. I waved back at her. She picked her way carefully among the rocks to join me, clutching her hat against the stiff ocean breeze.

"You were napping," I said. "I didn't want to disturb you."

She squinted at the boats in the distance. "It's a pleasant view, though a bit windy for my taste. Isn't June still too cold for sea-bathing?" She gestured toward my sodden bathing costume.

"I find the water quite bracing. And I had the entirety of the sea to myself. Well, at least this corner of it." I combed out my hair with my fingers and began twisting it into an expedient topknot.

She watched me with a skeptical eye. "I take it the conversation with your mother didn't go well."

Cassie, bless her, knows me well enough to discern when my craving for solitude and physical activity means I'm feeling unsettled.

I finished pinning my hair and started to wring out my hem. The warmth of the late-afternoon sun felt good upon my back and was drying out the rest of me nicely. "It went as well as could be expected, I suppose."

"What did she want?"

I recounted the bare bones of our conversation, including Mother's discovery of my current employment—at which my friend drew a sharp breath of surprise—the anonymous note, and the possibility that it was written out of spite by Bridget's friend.

Cassie pursed her lips as she considered it. "A jilted girl with a grudge makes the most sense, Pen. It stretches the bounds of logic to think that Collinsworth could have pushed his wife off a cliff without anyone seeing him do it, and get away with it since."

"I know," I conceded. "But one of the reasons I came here to bathe was to survey this part of the Cliff Walk. Mother doesn't have the details regarding Eunice Collinsworth's accident. She heard it was somewhere along the path, presumably along a treacherous section of it. I haven't encountered any such terrain, but there's more of the Walk—the housekeeper tells me it's a three-mile stretch, from Easton Beach to the north of us and then down to Bailey's Beach."

"So your first task will be to find out more about Eunice Collinsworth's death?" Cassie asked. "A rather awkward inquiry, particularly with Bridget on the brink of becoming the *second* Mrs. Collinsworth."

I blew out a breath, hoping Mother's prognostication that I'd make matters worse was off the mark.

We returned in time to dress for dinner.

"When is your father supposed to arrive?" Cassie asked, as we climbed the stairs to our room. The east wing of the cottage was being made ready for the influx of guests due to arrive the night before the wedding, so we were to share the last of the bedrooms in the west wing.

"I haven't had the chance to ask. I assume he's occupied with work."

Papa had always been the more distant parent of the two, caring about me in a preoccupied sort of way. Perhaps I was one of his hobbies—hunting pheasant, building model ships, and raising a daughter. On the positive side, my elopement hadn't distressed him as greatly as it had my mother. It would be good to see him again.

We'd changed into our dinner frocks and Cassie was putting the finishing touches to my hair—still slightly damp—when there was a knock. The maid came in with a basket.

"'Scuse me, Miss Hamilton," she said with a bob, "this jes' came for you." She handed it over and closed the door behind her.

"What beautiful flowers." I freed the carefully wrapped vase of hydrangeas from the basket, admiring the mix of blues and pinks. A card was attached.

I was busy reading the note when Cassie, rummaging through the rest of the basket, laughed aloud. "Why on earth would someone send us a tin of coffee?" She held up a square canister wrapped in speckled-blue paper, stamped *Mrs. Acker's Morning Blend Coffee.*

I tapped the note. "It's a souvenir from my bank adventure." I read it aloud:

Dear Miss Hamilton,

Forgive me for presuming to write you when we have not been formally introduced, but Mr. Fisher at the First National Bank of Newport apprised me of your aid today in rescuing my man Tompkins from the machinations of a sneak thief.

Please accept these flowers as a token of my gratitude, along with the coffee that Tompkins left behind. I am not in need of it, but thought you might enjoy it.

Your servant,

CHAPTER 4

*T*he long, mahogany dining room table was draped in a richly gold-embroidered white cloth and set in high style for the occasion, with rose-and-fern arrangements, gleaming crystal goblets, and gold charger plates that shone in the light of three sets of tall candelabras. It was going to get warm in here quickly.

The Revered Chester, a man with a high, domed forehead and an avuncular air, gallantly helped Mother into her chair at one end of the table while he presided at the other. Reg Collinsworth was paired across the table from his bride-to-be, of course. From my short observation of him thus far he seemed a pleasant, well-mannered fellow, and obviously enamored of Bridget. He was clean-shaven and certainly handsome—dark, wavy hair carefully smoothed back with pomade, clear, dark eyes below wide brows, and the chiseled cheekbones and jawline that young ladies tend to swoon over.

His friend, Maxwell Trent, seemed close in age to his friend —late twenties by my estimate. He didn't have Collinsworth's striking features—his medium-brown straight hair, mustache, and fawn-brown eyes were frankly unremarkable—but he possessed an easygoing graciousness that made him immediately likable. Certainly in Rebecca Blakely's admiring eyes, and naturally he was paired with her at the table.

As we were sorely lacking in male company, that left the remaining three ladies—Cassie, myself, and Collinsworth's sister Grace—seated along the middle sides of the table. Not surprising—it is indeed the metaphorical middle ground to which unpaired females of a "certain age," as it is delicately put, have long been relegated in society. Cassie sat beside me and Grace was directly across, with her brother on one side and Trent upon the other. I found it an ideal placement for my purposes. I could converse with Collinsworth's sister without directly engaging the object of my inquiry and yet keep my eye upon him all the while.

Although a spinster and in her early forties, Grace Collinsworth didn't look the part. She had undoubtedly been a beauty in her prime. Even now, her delicate brow, lightly lined forehead, deep cheekbones, and full lips carried the appeal of lingering youth. She possessed lustrous chestnut-brown hair with just a tinge of silver at the temples.

The soup course was being removed by the time I asked my first question. "So, Miss Collinsworth, I understand you and your brother are native to Newport?"

She turned toward me. Her warm, brown eyes gave one the sense that she was taking your full measure, all in a glance. "Indeed, I've lived here all my life."

"Do you travel much?" Cassie inquired.

"Reginald, of course, travels widely." She gave her brother an affectionate glance. "I, however, prefer to keep close to home, except for visiting the occasional gallery or attending a concert in New York."

Collinsworth smiled at his sister. "Who needs to travel when the handsome society fellows come to one's doorstep every summer?" His eyes took on a mischievous glint. "Especially that Count fellow—what's his name?"

"Count de Claes," she said shortly.

"Right—de Claes," Collinsworth said. "Funny little fellow. German, I think. He seems quite taken with you."

Miss Collinsworth's cheeks pinkened as she sipped from her water glass.

"This is my first visit to Newport," I said, in an attempt to rescue her from her brother's teasing.

Her eyes brightened in interest. "Really? Where does the Hamilton family spend its summers, if I might inquire?"

My mother overheard the question. "We have a cottage in the Hamptons. The area is not as commercialized as is Newport."

Before the lady had time to bristle at the remark, I asked, "What local sights would you recommend, Miss Collinsworth? I took a stroll along a bit of your Cliff Walk today."

Out of the corner of my eye, I saw Mother wince.

"Ah!" the Reverend Chester said brightly. He peered over his pewter-rimmed spectacles in our direction. "I take my morning constitutional along there. Lovely views. Stretches for more than three miles, you know. We're in the northern part of it, where the walking is easier. Down at the southern tip, it becomes exceedingly rocky and difficult to navigate. One must be especially careful there, as it's easy to lose one's footing…." His voice trailed off as both Collinsworth and his sister shot him a look. He cleared his throat. "*Hum*, well. I beg your pardon."

I adopted an innocent, bewildered expression.

"You could not know," Grace Collinsworth began, with a quick glance at her brother, "as you are a stranger to these parts, but our family suffered a tragedy along the Cliff Walk."

I tipped my head in apology. "I do not mean to intrude, of course, but what tragedy is that? So that I do not inadvertently distress you in the future," I added.

Collinsworth reached over and patted his sister's arm. "Grace is being overly delicate about the matter. Nearly two years have passed. It was distressing at the time, naturally, but we are past that now. You see, Miss Hamilton, my first wife, Eunice, fell from the Cliff Walk and died from her injuries."

Bridget kept her gaze fixed upon her plate. Mother glared in my direction and gripped her roll so tightly I wondered if she would have stuffed it in my mouth to keep me from prolonging the conversation. But there was no stopping it now.

"How unfortunate," Cassie interjected. "Where along the Walk did it happen? I do hope we won't encounter such treacherous terrain during our local ramblings."

Bless the girl, she'd asked the question that I could not.

The Reverend Chester chimed in, "You won't have to worry, my dear. As long as you keep to the path you'll be right as rain. Poor Mrs. Collinsworth was apparently off the Walk, scrambling among the outcropping just near the Forty Steps. The rocks there are quite slippery when the tide comes in." His eyes took on a faraway look. "I recall in '78, a boy was fishing down there and got swept right out! The fellow who jumped in to rescue him drowned, too...." Noticing Mother's withering look, he subsided into silence.

I dearly wanted to ask what the Forty Steps were, but Mother had now turned her sharp eyes and hooked nose in my direction. It was time for a well-ordered retreat. "What other diversions do you enjoy here, Miss Collinsworth?" I asked instead.

Mother looked away to butter her roll.

"We have Fort Days now that it's summertime," the lady answered. "The army is stationed at Fort Adams, you know. There is a dress parade and the regimental band plays in the afternoons."

Rebecca Blakely reached for her glass. "Of far more interest is the evening promenade. Everyone who is anyone in Newport —the best families of the Register—take a drive along the picturesque stretch of Bellevue Avenue to both see and be seen." She sat back with a sigh. "At least, that's what I hear. I haven't yet gone."

Maxwell Trent, who hadn't engaged in the general conversation up to this point, leaned toward the young lady. "You should most certainly go, Miss Blakely. "You'd see some of the smartest equipages in these parts. Bennett's new cabriolet looks to be the fastest of the bunch, though frankly he'll race anything he happens to be driving. He'll have a time of it trying to beat my phaeton, though, and Reeves is green with envy about it. He's another friend of ours," Trent clarified, no doubt noting Cassie's frown. "He couldn't be here tonight—had some tiresome reception to attend. Poor fellow—first the Matthewses and now the Latts. Eligible bachelors can barely get an evening to themselves in the summertime." He winked at Collinsworth. "Good thing I'm your best man. Best excuse in the world to get out of tedious gatherings."

But the identity of Mr. Reeves wasn't the source of Cassie's grimace. "Surely, sir, you do not *race* your vehicles along a public avenue?" she asked.

Collinsworth lowered his eyes briefly in a sheepish look as Trent replied with enthusiasm, "Of course! Bennett's always throwing down some wager or other. He's ready to race anyone and anything. Don't worry—we stay out of everyone's way." His cheek dimpled in an out-and-out boyish grin.

"Or they stay out of yours," Grace Collinsworth muttered.

"In fact," Trent said, ignoring her and turning back to Rebecca Blakely, "I'd enjoy the chance to show you my phaeton. It's a real beauty. Twelve-spoke wheels, red-velvet seat—and the suspension! Such a comfortable ride. We can join the promenade tomorrow evening, if you'd like."

The girl brightened. "Oh, how fun!"

Mother frowned. "I'm not sure that's appropriate, Rebecca. Heaven knows what your mother would say if I allowed it."

Bridget, whose mood had begun to improve considerably since we'd abandoned the ghoulish topic of the first Mrs. Collinsworth's demise, spoke up. "It's an open-air vehicle, Aunt

Honoria, and there are lots of people about. It's all perfectly respectable."

Reg Collinsworth leaned in. "If you like, Mrs. Hamilton, we can ride behind Trent's conveyance and keep an eye on them. Bridget and I have wanted to try out my new surrey along Bellevue."

Mother's skeptical frown turned nearly comical. "And who will be watching the two of you, pray? You're not married yet."

"Well, we *are* an engaged couple," Bridget said, with a quiet smile for her fiancé, which was warmly reciprocated. "But it's easily remedied." She turned to me and Cassie. "Would you care to join us tomorrow evening? There's plenty of room."

Ah, another task for the spinsters—chaperoning young love. The thought of watching the preening elite seek to out-impress one another wasn't my idea of an evening's entertainment, but I agreed all the same, as did Cassie. I had one errand in mind before then, however.

"Is there a reading room or library hereabouts?" I asked. "Lord Ashton's house collection is rather—dry." I wasn't looking for leisure reading—I wanted to examine back issues of the local newspaper. Any library of significance would archive at least the past year of the neighborhood newspaper, and I hoped more than that.

"There's the Newport Reading Room," Collinsworth answered. "Even though it's membership-only, you need only mention you're staying at the Ashton cottage in order to get in. Lord Ashton is a patron of theirs. Of course, it's a rather stuffy establishment. Bennett tried to liven up the place back in '78"—

Trent interrupted with a chuckle. "I'll say! The old codgers are still getting over it. Bennett dared Sugar Candy—that's his polo chum who used to be in the cavalry—to ride his pony up the steps of the Reading Room. Candy did him one better and rode right through the entrance!"

Mother frowned, but Miss Blakely leaned forward in interest. "What happened then?"

"They banned Bennett from the Reading Room and withdrew his membership." Collinsworth waved a dismissive hand. "But that doesn't stop a fellow like him for long. Bennett got the upper hand by starting his own club, the Newport Casino Club."

Trent nodded. "Far better than any stuffy Reading Room. It's turning out to be quite a profitable enterprise. Wildly popular in the summer."

"Ah! That's where you're to be married, isn't it?" Cassie asked Collinsworth.

"You should see the place," he said. "Bennett has quite the set up. Banquet halls, courts for lawn tennis, bandstands—all sorts of entertainments."

James Gordon Bennett had become the stuff of legend among the locals, it seemed. Certainly Collinsworth and his fellows considered him a veritable paragon of manliness. I struggled to keep a straight face as I returned to the original subject. "How...interesting. Is the Reading Room open on Saturday mornings?"

Miss Collinsworth sniffed. "I'd say you'll find more material to your liking at the Redwood Library, Miss Hamilton. It, too, is a subscription library, though less exclusive. You should have no trouble borrowing what you wish. Lady Ashton is an avid patron. It's on Bellevue, near Touro Park. And they are open on Saturday mornings."

That seemed the better choice. The Newport Reading Room would no doubt be filled with patrons familiar with the Collinsworths. It would hardly do for gossip over my research to reach Reg Collinsworth's ears. A quiet request of the Redwood librarian who dealt with the general public was less likely to be broadcast.

I sat back to allow my dinner plate to be removed. "An excellent suggestion, Miss Collinsworth, thank you."

She smiled. "Do call me Grace. We are to be family now."

"Then you must call me Pen," I answered.

Across the table, Mother's frown deepened. I strongly suspected that my family status was confined to the duration of the case and nothing more.

CHAPTER 5

Saturday, June 18th

*T*he Redwood Library was an impressive structure, built in the eighteenth-century Georgian style, with its tall, white Doric columns and deep portico. Even at this early hour it was bustling with patrons. Most were female, running the gamut of young ladies who giggled behind gloved hands as they shared popular novels to matrons frowning through pince-nez over copies of Godey's *Ladies' Book*. A few gentlemen, including an elderly man wearing a Roman collar, were ensconced in comfortable chairs by the window, reading newspapers.

A stiff-necked, middle-aged clerk with an unmistakable air of officiousness approached. "May I pull something from the collections for you, miss?"

I noticed out of the corner of my eye that the priest, still clutching his copy of the—what was it?—ah, yes, the *Newport Daily News*, had stirred from his chair and was sidling closer.

"I wish to consult several back issues of the *Newport Daily News*," I said. "July and August of 1885, specifically. Do you possess copies that far back?"

"Of course. We keep an archive going back three years.

However, anything beyond the last six months is stored in boxes in the basement." He gave me a pointed look over his reading glasses. "It would be quite the endeavor to retrieve them."

"I regret the inconvenience, but I do need to consult those issues."

He narrowed his eyes. "For what purpose?"

"That is my own concern, and none of yours," I retorted.

"Now, now, Barney," the priest interrupted. His voice was more vigorous than I would have expected for a man of his advanced years, judging by his deeply lined face and what tufts of grizzled gray hair remained on his balding pate. "Let us be of help to the dear lady. Young Jimmy isn't doing anything at present, except looking at pictures in old magazines. He can help you shift boxes around. Should take no time at all." He glanced across the room and crooked a finger. A lad of ten, with a head full of wavy red hair and a gap-toothed grin, ran over to join us.

"Yes, Father?" he called out.

The clerk winced.

The priest tousled the child's head. "Now then, Jimmy, we mustn't run and yell inside a library. It's a lot like being in church, you know." He gestured to the clerk. "Mr. Burrows has a small task for you." He pulled out a penny and pressed it into the boy's palm, much to his delight.

With a sigh of resignation, the clerk led the boy to the stairs.

"Thank you, sir," I said to the priest.

He gave a short bow. "Father Kelly, at your service, Miss—?"

"Hamilton," I answered.

"Hamilton, eh?" He adjusted the paper under his arm and gestured to a pair of chairs. "Come, sit down. You may as well be comfortable. It could take a while."

"You are under no obligation to wait with me," I protested, as he sat down as well.

He waved off my objection. "I have to wait for Jimmy, anyway. I'm helping to keep him out from underfoot at his home this morning." He gave me a sideways glance. "I believe Jimmy's ma is the cook for your family, if I got your name right, dear."

"You mean Mrs. Mullins?" I asked in surprise. "I didn't realize she had children."

Five of them, in fact," he said. "Jimmy's the middle child."

Mercy, *five*? "How does she manage to work at the Ashton cottage?"

"Her eldest girl is sixteen and takes care o' the young ones, but Jimmy's been a particular nuisance to her lately. Bored, I 'spect. He goes with his ma to help in the Ashton kitchen sometimes, too. I'll be dropping him off there once the library closes at lunchtime."

"It's nice of you to take charge of him," I said.

He shrugged. "No trouble a'tall. And once the lawn tennis tournaments start up at the Club, he'll work there as a ball boy. That'll keep him plenty busy."

"You mean the Newport Club? My cousin's wedding will be held there next Saturday," I said. "I do hope these sporting competitions don't take place then." I couldn't imagine the chaos that a nearby athletic competition and its spectators would have upon a solemn wedding ceremony.

"A few more weeks, at least—ah! There's Barney now."

The clerk and the boy, each carrying a dusty box, approached the table. Father Kelly quickly cleared a space. Patrons seated at nearby desks looked up.

"One more box and that'll be the lot," the clerk said, mopping his forehead with his kerchief as Jimmy ran back toward the stairs—Father Kelly clucking his tongue at the boy's departing back.

I set aside my gloves to keep them clean and was elbow-deep in the boxes when Jimmy returned. Now, at close quarters, I could see the same freckled snub nose and animated green eyes as Mrs. Mullins. "Thank you, Jimmy." I added two more pennies to his collection.

The lad gave a whoop and hurried off.

The next two hours were occupied with sifting through the neatly folded newspapers, scanning headlines, and finally setting aside three issues. The first two were dated close to Eunice Collinsworth's death on July 10, 1885, and the third three weeks later.

Heedless of my filthy hands, I pulled out my notepad and pencil to transcribe the articles. The first was dated the day after her death.

TRAGEDY NEAR THE FORTY STEPS

The body of Mrs. Eunice Collinsworth, wife of Reginald Collinsworth, was found this morning in the water near the place along the Cliff Walk known as the Forty Steps.

Mr. George Bancroft, retired diplomat and scholar who summers at nearby Rosecliff, espied the unfortunate lady during his morning stroll. He quickly enlisted a nearby fisherman and his son to wade into the water and retrieve the body. Back at the Collinsworth home, an alarm had not yet been given for the missing lady, as her husband was out of town and the staff was not aware of her absence in the early morning hours.

The prevailing opinion is that Mrs. Collinsworth lost her footing during a late-night stroll, hit her head as she fell, and drowned. The authorities, of course, are looking into the particulars of the lady's death, but no foul play is suspected.

I made note of the reporter's name. Tucker Gannon. A local, I assumed. I hoped he still worked for the *Daily News*. Perhaps he could provide details that had not been included in the article. A chat with George Bancroft was worth pursuing as well.

I turned to the second article, dated six days after the first, written by the same reporter:

POLICE DETERMINE MRS. COLLINSWORTH'S
DEATH AN ACCIDENT

Today, the chief of police pronounced himself satisfied with the results of the department's investigation into last week's drowning of Mrs. Eunice Collinsworth, wife of investment banker and avid yachtsman Reginald Collinsworth. After exhaustive interviews with the entirety of the Collinsworth household, an inquiry of the locals who frequent the path, and a search of the house and grounds, no evidence has come to light to contradict the opinion that the unfortunate woman strayed from the path, fell to the rocks below, and perished.

The coroner clarified the manner of Mrs. Collinsworth's death, asserting that she did not drown. Instead, the wound to her head from hitting the rocks as she fell proved fatal before she reached the water.

A private funeral service for Mrs. Collinsworth is scheduled for this coming Tuesday.

I re-read the article several times. *She did not drown.* I was already skeptical of the woman leaving the path voluntarily in the dark and tumbling down the cliff face. Of course, she might have seen something close to shore that had aroused her curiosity, then slipped upon the wet rocks as she went to investigate. But would she have hit her head so hard upon impact that she was killed instantly? I wanted a look at the Forty Steps and surrounding terrain to determine what was feasible.

I turned to the last article, dated three weeks after her death and written by a different reporter. It related only indirectly to Mrs. Collinsworth.

WIDOWER IN MOURNING TO LEAVE NEWPORT EARLY

Reginald Collinsworth, a native of these parts, usually divides his time between business concerns in New York City and yachting here in Newport in the summer. However, the recent death of his beloved wife, Eunice, has understandably made it impossible for him to pursue pleasure-seeking. He is instead heading back to the city to take solace in work, as men who mourn are apt to do.

Mr. Collinsworth's sister, Miss Grace Collinsworth, will move back into the main residence and oversee the running of it during his absence.

The rest of the story I knew from there—Collinsworth had avoided Newport and its sad associations for the next year. Then he met Bridget, courted her, and decided to return here to wed. I wondered how Bridget felt about that.

But what I wondered most was how much Reg Collinsworth had inherited upon his wife's death, and what the state of his finances had been before the fact.

I was so lost in thought that it took me a moment to realize the librarian had been trying to catch my attention.

"Miss…miss…excuse me. It's the noon hour. Time to close."

"That late?" I flipped closed my notepad and futilely wiped my hands on my handkerchief before pulling on my gloves. "Thank you for your assistance."

He gave a chilly nod, his gaze raking over the stacks of newspapers and boxes to be cleaned up and put away.

I shaded my eyes against the glare of the sun as I stepped outside in search of a cab. Several patrons followed me out, scattering in different directions.

Except for one man who crossed the street into Touro Park and settled himself upon a bench. Although he kept the brim of his derby low and I couldn't see his eyes, I had the distinct feeling he was watching me. He was tall but slightly built, clean-shaven, with a bit of sandy-colored hair peeking out below his hat. He looked familiar somehow. A ripple of unease went up my spine.

A hansom pulled up. "The Cedars," I said, and climbed in. As we swung away from the curb, I peeked out the window. The man was hurrying back across the street in my direction.

My heart clenched. Was he trying to stop me?

But no—he turned down the street, away from the vehicle.

As we took the next corner I saw him no more. But I'd seen enough. I knew who he was, despite the fact that he'd shaved off his mustache in the meantime.

It was the sneak thief from the bank.

But why had he been following me?

CHAPTER 6

"This basket is heavy," Cassie puffed, shifting the handle.

I reached to take it from her. "We certainly won't starve with the generous lunch Mrs. Mullins packed."

The afternoon was perfect for a picnic, the sunlight shimmering upon the steel-gray water, the sky a boundless blue. The well-trodden path was bare of any growth save the occasional sturdy tuft of grass here and there. Below lay the rocks, mostly shale and sandstone, along with other varieties that Bridget could no doubt identify.

But it would not do to bring Bridget with us today. Not when I was trying to figure out if her fiancé had murdered his first wife near this spot.

We stopped when we came upon the Forty Steps, an iron staircase which connected the cluster of estates off Narragansett Avenue with the Cliff Walk and the water's edge below. The steps were intersected by a viewing platform where several ladies in wide-brimmed hats and frilly parasols lingered. They nodded as we passed.

We picked our way carefully to reach the shoreline and spread our blanket upon a smooth, wide rock a little distance away from a group of men fishing with their sons.

Papa flexed his arm to grasp mine more tightly. "I'm sorry to hear it, my dear."

Fortunately, he didn't ask for any details. Bless his soul—he'd never much involved himself in the particulars of the "feminine sphere," as he called it.

Of course, there are times when one is compelled to become involved in female affairs, and the Collinsworth matter was one of them.

"Papa, what do you know about Reg Collinsworth?" I asked, after he'd greeted Cassie and taken the basket. I let go of his arm to walk beside him on the path, Cassie following behind. "I understand you looked into his background when he asked permission to marry Bridget."

Papa stifled a sigh. "Your mother said she wanted you to look into the accusation in that anonymous note, though she didn't tell me why she asked you in particular. It seems a sordid business for a young woman to get mixed up in."

So, Mother hadn't told him I was a private detective. Interesting.

"Given the acrimony between the two of you," he went on, "I never imagined you would accede to her request."

"The decision wasn't an easy one," I observed dryly. "What can you tell me about Collinsworth?"

"He's a well-educated fellow. Harvard, you know. Junior partner in a Wall Street firm."

"Does he need to work for his living, then?"

"Not anymore, that's for certain. Eunice Collinsworth left him a tidy sum upon her death, God rest her soul."

"Do you know anything of his finances before that?" I asked.

"I don't think there was anything nefarious going on, if that's what you mean," he answered. "He wasn't a pauper by any means when he married Eunice. His mansion here in Newport—Gull's Bluff, it's called—is impressive, and there was a townhouse in New York City as well, I believe, though that might have been Eunice's…I can't recall."

"One man's opinion of 'enough' may not be another's," I pointed out. "Mother said you checked into his affairs before giving him your blessing to marry Bridget. Is he an extravagant spender?"

"There was one extravagance—he bought a yacht just after he married his first wife. But what young man wouldn't, particularly to show off to one's friends?"

"Show off to his friends?" I echoed.

"Trent and Reeves, fellows he knows from his college days. Those two are always underfoot. Lay-abouts, if you ask me. Not quite sure what they do for a living, as it seems most of their time is occupied with chasing amusements at Collinsworth's expense."

"Really? I met Trent last night, but the other fellow—Reeves —had not been in attendance."

"Trent is the more mature of the two," Papa said, "but I had to show them both the door at a dinner party last month. Reeves couldn't hold his liquor, and both he and Trent had grown quarrelsome. I had a word with Reg afterward about cutting back on the time he spends with those two. Especially once he's married to our Bridget."

"Oh?" Cassie chimed in. "What was Collinsworth's reaction?"

"Seemed rather abashed about it all. At heart, he's a good man. He struggles with a bit of pride when it comes to keeping up appearances before his peers. He'll grow out of it."

I hoped so.

We stepped off the path to the drive in front of the cottage just as an expressman's wagon pulled away from the house.

"So many comings and goings when there's a wedding," Papa muttered.

Inside, Bridget and Miss Blakely were helping Mother unpack a number of wooden crates.

"Wedding gifts are beginning to arrive, isn't that exciting?" Rebecca Blakely said in a high-pitched voice. She brushed off the sawdust still clinging to a package wrapped in gold foil and gave an experimental shake. "Either a mantel clock or a gravy boat, I'd say."

Bridget burst out laughing as she eyed the package. "A very *large* gravy boat."

Papa surveyed the sprawl of crates, filler, boxes and bows that had taken over the entryway. "*Must* they be delivered to the cottage? After all, the gifts are to be displayed at the reception. Can they not go directly to the Newport Club?"

"And entrust the safekeeping of valuable items to the staff of the Newport Club for an entire week?" Mother retorted. "Thefts happen all the time. Far better for the gifts to stay in the cottage for now. Besides, we need to catalogue them for the thank-you notes and determine how to best arrange them for display. More will be coming in the next few days."

He rolled his eyes and turned in the direction of the study, no doubt to escape the chaos and smoke his pipe in peace.

I dearly wished I could retreat along with him—minus the pipe—but Mother had other plans. "Penelope, you and Cassie find the housekeeper and arrange for a long table to be set up in the parlor. Draped in the best white linen cloths they have, if you please."

CHAPTER 7

*T*hat evening, as we were preparing to leave for the Bellevue Avenue promenade, I finally met Donald Reeves, the other "lay-about fellow" Papa had mentioned. I'd been in search of a maid to procure long hatpins—the ridiculously large-plumed hat I'd borrowed from Bridget needed additional anchoring—and I nearly bumped into him as he emerged from the kitchen.

"I beg your pardon!" he exclaimed, following me out to the foyer, where the rest of our party waited. Collinsworth performed the introductions.

Reeves was an agreeable-looking fellow, with clear gray eyes, a full head of wavy, reddish-brown hair, and a well-trimmed beard to match. Although he seemed a bit startled by my height —I was a good head taller—he nonetheless bowed over my hand politely. "A pleasure, Miss Hamilton."

"Where'd you get to, Reeves?" Collinsworth asked. "I turned around and you were gone."

Reeves grinned. "Got hungry and cadged a scone from your cook."

Maxwell Trent, who had been assisting Miss Blakely with

her wrap, chuckled. "Always looking for that little bit extra, eh, Don?"

Was there an edge to Trent's light-hearted comment? His mild expression revealed little.

Reeves gave a good-natured shrug. "As do you, Max. Reg lives much better than we do."

Collinsworth spread his hands. "What's mine is yours, gentlemen."

"Not quite," Bridget muttered.

"Ah, that reminds me." Trent reached into his pocket. "You left your onyx cufflinks at my place last week." He passed them to Collinsworth.

"I was wondering where they'd gotten to." Collinsworth gave Reeves a mischievous look. "Thought you might have them, you'd admired them so."

Reeves spread his hands in mock innocence. "A fellow helps himself to a few Havanas and suddenly he's a jewel thief."

Bridget made a face. "You're welcome to the cigars." She glanced at her fiancé. "I don't care for their smell at all."

"I hardly notice it." Collinsworth clasped her hand. "But of course, my dear, if you find them objectionable, I shall stop immediately."

Trent and Reeves exchanged a sniggering look.

Rebecca Blakely gave an impatient flutter of her rose-embroidered silk fan. "Is Miss Leigh coming down? We should get going."

"I'm afraid she has a headache from too much sun today," I said. "She asked me to pass along her regrets."

"All right, then," Collinsworth said, "shall we?" He turned to Reeves as we crossed the drive and made our way to the waiting vehicles. "There's more room for you in our vehicle now. You won't have to be crammed in the jump seat behind Trent and Miss Blakely."

"Delighted," Reeves murmured. He shot a look in Miss Blakely's direction as Trent settled her into his vehicle and solicitously helped tuck her skirts, parasol, and fan. No doubt that young lady's company in close quarters had been the preferred option, even if he'd have to compete with Trent for her attentions.

Collinsworth helped Bridget into the surrey, leaving Reeves to assist me into the back seat. Not an easy operation—our female finery privileged form over function, as it is often wont to do. I had not managed to procure more pins for my top-heavy hat, drat it, and now I could feel it listing to one side, the plume tickling Reeves's ear.

The procession of open-air vehicles was well underway by the time we turned onto Bellevue Avenue. The most costly equipages I'd ever seen in one place rolled along the wide street, several emblazoned with peerage coat-of-arms. Some were driven by coachmen in brass-buttoned livery, others by top-hatted gentlemen such as Collinsworth, sporting the standard attire of his tribe—elegant morning coat, pinstripe vest, and precisely tied cravat. Ribbons and plumes larger than my own were in profusion here—on horses, on ladies, and even adorning the ill-behaved lap dogs that yipped at everyone who passed.

We rolled past sprawling, columned villas with sweeping stone driveways, past sidewalks populated with parasoled ladies who strolled to admire and be admired. As we approached the seaside boarding houses of the working folk on holiday, I could see men in rolled-up shirtsleeves leaning over the upper decks, chatting and smoking as they eyed the display.

"A finely matched pair of bays you have there, Mr. Collinsworth," I observed.

He glanced back briefly. "Why thank you, Miss Hamilton. Beautiful, aren't they?"

Reeves' nostrils flared in annoyance. "I'd been looking out for just such a pair for ages, but Reg here scooped them up, right out from under me."

Collinsworth laughed. "Come now. I outbid you, fair and square."

"Is it my fault you have deeper pockets?" Reeves retorted.

Collinsworth's back stiffened, though he made no reply.

Reeves' face smoothed in an easygoing expression. "Now, now—just teasing you, old fellow." His gaze shifted to Bridget, sitting beside her fiancé on the velvet-padded driver's bench, and his voice dropped to a murmur. "You always do seem to get everything you want, all too easily."

Even a child could read the underlying current of such an interchange, but it raised more questions than it clarified. Had Reeves been a rival for Bridget's affections, or was his remark one of general envy? There were certainly cracks in this camaraderie. Could Reeves have sent the anonymous note?

Bridget might know more about how well the two got along, and Trent as well. In fact, I had quite a bit to ask my cousin when we had a quiet moment to ourselves. Of course, how Collinsworth and his friends dealt with each other was not what Mother had asked me to investigate. Still, it might help me better understand Bridget's husband-to-be.

We'd been following behind Trent's conveyance all the while. When the crush of vehicles finally thinned as we left the fashionable section, Trent's horse stepped up to a brisk trot.

"Looks like he's continuing toward the south shore," Collinsworth said, picking up the pace himself. "Now you'll have a better idea of what this fine pair of horses can really do."

"There's a lovely view of the bay and the islands farther along this stretch," Bridget said over her shoulder. She dropped her voice and leaned in toward her fiancé. "Not so fast, dear."

At that moment, the clatter of wheels and a flash of red and black caught my eye. A landau was drawing abreast of us, the single driver a man of middling age dressed in fine evening attire. He slapped the reins with abandon and tipped his hat to us as he raced past.

Collinsworth's back stiffened. "Damnation, Bennett," he growled, "you can see I have ladies here!"

Bennett? The man was living up to his reckless reputation.

Collinsworth whipped up his horses in pursuit.

Reeves hooted in delight as he leaned forward briefly and clapped his friend upon the shoulder. "That's right, Reg, don't let him beat ya this time!"

As we clung to the sides for dear life, Bridget using her best, Honoria-inspired voice to command her fiancé to stop—to no avail—we passed Maxwell Trent's vehicle. He'd, at least, had the good sense to pull over. He and Miss Blakely gaped at us as we whizzed by.

I barely had breath to speak as the wind blew in my face and tore at my hat. I struggled to hold on to hat and seat simultaneously. The latter soon became impossible when we hit a bump in the road—this section was not as well maintained as the stretch which fronted the pricey villas—and I landed in Reeves's lap. "I beg your pardon," I murmured.

"Not at all, my dear." He grinned amiably as I scrambled to re-seat myself.

Collinsworth was gaining on Bennett's vehicle, and he let out a gleeful whoop as we drew up to his adversary. "Any time, any*where*, Bennett!" he called tauntingly.

I turned to get a good look at the man as we passed, but in the process lost grip of my hat. It sailed behind us, landing—to my mixed dismay and amusement—squarely in his face.

The moment turned more alarming as Bennett tried to swat it away and inadvertently steered his horses toward us. The animals veered at the last minute, pivoting the front wheel of his equipage directly into our rear wheel, which broke off and sent us skidding into a ditch.

I couldn't distinguish my own shrieks from everyone else's. Let us suffice to say that a good bit of shrieking commenced, mingled with a number of ungentlemanly oaths. By the time we'd begun sorting out tumbled seat cushions, upturned skirts, and lost shoes, and had thankfully established that no one—including the horses—had suffered grievous injury, Trent and Miss Blakely had caught up to us on the road.

Bennett pulled over farther ahead, jumped off, and approached to render aid.

I got my first good look at the man idolized by Collinsworth and his set. He might be a social colossus but he was certainly not a physical one, being of average height and build. Beneath his prominent nose he sported a luxurious light-brown mustache but was otherwise clean-shaven.

His heavy-lidded, blue eyes— the sort of blue one perceives beneath a layer of ice—flicked over the sad scene. "Ah, what a shame—Collinsworth, isn't it? How may I be of assistance?"

Reg Collinsworth stiffened. "You deliberately rammed my surrey! Most unsporting, sir!"

"That, my dear fellow, was not my doing. An item of female frippery was thrown in my face as you passed." He glared in my direction. "Needless to say, one cannot drive properly when brushing aside an enormous ostrich plume."

All eyes turned to me at that moment. I gathered what remnants of dignity I could—no easy task when one is still missing a shoe. "Had I known I was to participate in a street race, sir, I would have brought my goggles and duster and left the fripperies at home."

Miss Blakely, who was helping Bridget brush off her skirt, put a hand to her mouth to unsuccessfully suppress a snort.

Bennett's mustache twitched. "Fair enough." He walked over to the ditch, retrieved my shoe and the infamous hat, presenting them to me with a bow. "I don't believe we've met, miss. Gordon Bennett, at your service."

"Penelope Hamilton," I answered.

"Indeed?" He frowned. "Where have I heard the name before?"

I put on my shoe—the hat was a lost cause—and straightened. "The episode at the bank. Thank you for the flowers. And the coffee."

"Now I remember. Lady Ashton mentioned you as well, I

believe, but I can't quite recall…it was at one of her tiresome soirees." He tapped his chin thoughtfully.

Mentally cursing Lady Ashton's loose tongue, and hoping to stave off any detective talk, I quickly interjected, "You may be thinking of the Hamilton family as a whole. Lady Ashton generously offered the use of her cottage, as we prepare for my cousin's upcoming nuptials."

His wide forehead smoothed. "That must be it. And I understand the wedding is to take place at my club." He gave a short bow in Bridget's direction. "My congratulations, Miss Sinclair"—his glance flicked to Collinsworth—"though *good luck* might be the more proper term."

Bridget gave a chilly smile.

Trent, who'd been hovering near Miss Blakely all the while, turned aside in a fit of coughing.

"Well now," Bennett said, glancing over his shoulder as several vehicles slowed and gawked, "we can't stand here all evening in the middle of the road. You are all invited back to my home to rest and recuperate from the experience. Since this gentleman's phaeton"—he gestured to Trent—"is insufficient to accommodate you all, may I suggest that I take Miss Hamilton and Miss Sinclair in my vehicle. You can come along too—who are you? Ah, Reeves—unless you want to wait here with your friend. I'll send my mechanic here to tend to your wheel, Collinsworth. Once it's repaired, you can join us." He spread his hands in a conciliatory gesture. "I'll feed you all a late, *al fresco* supper by way of apology."

Trent and Reeves brightened.

Collinsworth was still in sulks, but no doubt recognized the practicality of the plan. "All right, then," he muttered.

His mood was in no way improved by Bridget, who refused to even look in his direction. I'd never seen her in such a cold rage, but who could blame her? Her fiancé's recklessness could have had far worse consequences. Collinsworth attempted to help her into Bennett's vehicle, but she wordlessly shook off his hand and climbed in without a backward glance.

Each of Collinsworth's fellows were abandoning him, Reeves getting into the driver's seat next to Bennett, and Trent following behind in his own vehicle. I could understand why Trent did not stay behind, as he had Miss Blakely with him and was obliged to see her comfortably settled. But Reeves, who had egged on Collinsworth to begin with, seemed to feel no compunction about leaving his friend to wait by his lonesome for aid to arrive. As we pulled away I watched Collinsworth, hands in pockets, eyeing his damaged axle with a gloomy expression. I almost felt sorry for him.

CHAPTER 8

*O*ur first view of Gordon Bennett's mansion, Stone Villa, promised everything one might expect of the home of a wealthy newspaper owner, yachtsman, and overall hedonist, if accounts of him were to be believed. We passed through gates whose posts were each topped with a large owl figurine— denoting Bennett's major commercial enterprise, the *New York Herald*—and approached the sprawling fieldstone-and-granite Italianate manor house.

Bennett tossed the reins to a waiting attendant and jumped down. "See to their comfort, I must speak to Jack at the carriage house—" He broke off as a man dressed in a plain black suit and bowler hat emerged from a side door. "Ah, I thought you'd left already."

I recognized the fellow as Tompkins, who'd nearly been robbed at the bank.

Tompkins inclined his head deferentially. "No indeed, sir, I had to give the laundress instructions on your shirts." He caught sight of me and lifted his hat in recognition. "Hello, miss." He eyed the rest of our group and turned back to his master. "Have you changed your plans? If you have need of me, I'll stay."

"No, no, man, enjoy your Saturday night off."

"Thank you, sir." Tompkins turned to go. "I may still catch the last musicale performance of the evening."

Bennett chuckled at his valet's departing back. "More likely, scare up a game of Euchre and fleece the tourists at Perry House."

A perceptive maid, no doubt observing the windblown appearance of Bridget and myself, ushered us into a ladies' cloakroom while Trent and Reeves headed for the patio. Miss Blakely came with us to help.

"Reg will be the death of me," Bridget grumbled, as soon as the door closed behind us. She sat down on a vanity stool in front of a long mirror.

Miss Blakely's blue eyes clouded with disapproval. "He should certainly know better. I was relieved that Maxwell—I mean, Mr. Trent—elected to pull over and stay out of it."

"Thank heaven for that." Bridget eyed her reflection and began rearranging pins. "But be warned, Becky—Trent has gotten into some scrapes, too. If you plan to spend more time with him, you should keep that in mind."

Miss Blakely bristled. "I find that hard to believe."

"He's more level-headed than Reeves, I grant you," Bridget answered.

The image of Reeves egging on his friend in an endeavor that could have gotten us killed was painfully fresh. I pulled all the pins out of my hair and reached for a comb on the toiletries tray. I may as well start over.

"Here, let me help you," Miss Blakely offered. I passed her the comb as my mind raced over the possibilities. How suggestible was Collinsworth? Could he have been "egged on" to murder his first wife for her money? I dearly wanted to ask Bridget what she might know.

A welcome sight was the sideboard set up in Bennett's dining room, laden with delicate sandwiches, all manner of pastries, fresh fruit, cool lemonade and punch. A maid in a black dress, starched white apron, and cap stood waiting to serve us. I gratefully accepted a sandwich and glass of lemonade and went outside to the patio where the others had gathered, Bennett now among them.

He detached himself from the gentlemen and helped me into a chair. "I see you are tidy and more comfortable now, Miss Hamilton." He motioned to the chair across from me. "May I?"

"Of course."

The sun had already set. His expression was difficult to read in the light of the patio torches, making his eyes more hooded and emphasizing the hollows beneath. It was obvious that something was on his mind, however.

"The man who attempted to rob my valet at the bank," he began. "You don't know him, by any chance?"

I sat back in surprise. "Know him? Not at all. What makes you think so?"

He ignored the question and asked another. "Are you aware he's been following you?"

I gaped at him a good long minute, trying to gather my thoughts. "I'm aware of one such instance, but I cannot account for it."

"I see." His voice was tinged with disappointment.

I had so many questions it was difficult to know where to start. "How do you know he was following me? And how did you learn of it so quickly?"

"Someone broke into my villa last night."

Bennett was skilled at the art of the *non sequitur*, I'll give him that. Deciding to humor him in hopes that we would eventually circle back to my question, I said, "Have you called the police?"

"Nothing was stolen. I prefer to avoid further intrusion by handling it myself. Do a bit of investigating."

"Oh? What have you determined thus far?" I asked.

"I thought back to yesterday," he said. "The only other unusual event was Tompkins's experience at the bank. That's when I began to wonder about a possible connection between the sneak thief, the break in here—and *you*." He waited, no doubt expecting an outburst of female indignation.

Instead, I was intrigued. I could see where he could be going with this. "So you had my movements monitored—how? By bribing a cabbie or express driver, perhaps? Very efficient."

He blinked.

When he said nothing, I went on, "You wondered if I was in league with the sneak thief, and suspected I might have been warning him off at the bank rather than trying to interfere in his endeavors."

"The thought had crossed my mind," he said reluctantly.

"Naturally. And in the process of tracking my activities, you learned that a man—similar in description to the sneak thief—had been trailing me today." My cab driver could have told him that.

Bennett's eyes narrowed. "What were you searching for at the Redwood Library?"

"A needle in a haystack, Mr. Bennett," I retorted. It didn't surprise me that he'd found that out, too. The aggrieved librarian had undoubtedly been eager to describe the inconvenience I'd put him to. "Now, it is your turn to be more forthcoming, sir."

He glanced over his shoulder at Miss Blakely, Bridget, Reeves, and Trent conversing close by. "Let me show you the rose garden, Miss Hamilton. It's beautiful in the moonlight."

I would normally be reluctant to accede to a suggestion by a man with such a reputation as he, but I knew an assignation was not on his mind. "Very well."

"Miss Hamilton is eager to see the rose garden. We'll be back shortly," Bennett called over his shoulder as he guided me by the elbow down the stone steps. Even with my back to them, I heard one of the men snicker.

The rose garden was indeed beautiful. There is something about the night air that coaxes the flowers to release their perfume more sweetly than by day. As Bennett and I strode along the well-tended gravel paths between rows, I wished Cassie could be here. She would appreciate it more than I, identifying the varieties by scent alone.

"You said nothing was taken," I said, getting back to the matter at hand. "Are you sure?"

He gave a grunt of impatience. "I have already said as much."

"Where did the thief concentrate his efforts? Have you a safe?"

"The safe wasn't touched, but he'd obviously searched my bedroom and study along with Tompkins's quarters. We were out late and made the sad discovery when we returned."

"I see. You suspect Tompkins was the target. You've questioned your valet about it, I trust?"

"Indeed. He says it made no sense. I can see his point. Once the easy crime of opportunity at the bank was no longer possible, why would a thief risk breaking into a well-protected house for whatever cash he saw my valet withdraw?"

"True," I said, "though 'well-protected' may not be entirely accurate. The thief got in, after all. How did he accomplish that?"

"I'll show you."

I followed him to the partially embedded hatch of what looked to be a root cellar, now sporting a shiny new lock. I crouched down for a better look.

"This is one of my wine cellars," Bennett explained. "The padlock was cut"—

—"with nippers," I finished, pointing at the scratches upon the hasp. "And the inner door of the wine cellar—is it a simple latch, or did he have to pick the lock to access the house interior?"

I was so absorbed in the hunt for clues that I'd quite forgotten myself.

Bennett scowled down at me. "You seem extraordinarily familiar with such matters. Who *are* you?"

I straightened and, with my height, I had the advantage of him by several inches. Not that this intimidated Mr. Gordon Bennett in the least, but it did wonders for my own determination to brazen it out. I was still hoping he'd been too bored—or too intoxicated—at Lady Ashton's soiree to remember the woman's gossip about me. "I am Penelope Hamilton, lately of Chicago, Illinois, and daughter of Curtis and Honoria Hamilton. I have a brain, Mr. Bennett, and I read the newspapers. Such knowledge on my part is not so astonishing."

"*Hum*, well…I suppose."

"We should rejoin the others," I said.

He took a step closer. "Afraid I shall compromise you, Miss Hamilton?"

"You're not my type," I snapped.

He shrugged good-naturedly and we turned back toward the sound of merry voices on the patio.

"Speaking of type," he said, "what is your cousin about, marrying Collinsworth? She could do better."

"Perhaps. What is it about the man that gives you pause?"

He sighed. "I have no special information. It's just that he doesn't seem particularly…mature. Oh, I know what you're thinking," he added, at the sound of my snort, "I'm not marriage material, either. The difference is I do not aspire to the marital state, and I wonder at Collinsworth giving it another go."

This looked to be an excellent opening. "That's right—his first wife died a couple of years ago. A tragic accident, I heard."

He nodded. "Along the Cliff Walk."

"I've walked that path. It's fairly well frequented. But I understand she wasn't found until morning. Don't you find that surprising?"

He gave me a puzzled look. "Granted it's a popular spot, particularly at the Forty Steps. In the evenings, servants from nearby establishments like to take their breaks there. But servants don't have a lot of leisure, you know, and no one knows when the lady decided to get some air."

"But the path itself is not hazardous. How did she fall from it?" I asked.

"I have no idea." His voice was tinged with impatience. "Why the questions? A rather ghoulish line of inquiry, though I've found such a thing common among the fairer sex."

I didn't rise to the jibe. "I merely wish to understand the circumstances."

"To what end? If you truly suspect Collinsworth of murder, then by all means, don't allow your cousin to marry him. But let the dead sleep in peace."

Do the dead sleep in peace when their murderers go free? I suspected not, but kept the thought to myself.

CHAPTER 9

*A*s it had been a long evening, the party broke up a short while after Reg Collinsworth joined us and had a bite to eat. He seemed as eager as the rest of us to leave after that.

I sat in the back seat of his newly repaired conveyance as Bridget and Collinsworth carried on a whispered argument in the front. But I paid little attention to them. My own thoughts were occupied with the problem of the blond-haired sneak thief. Had he indeed been the one to break into Bennett's cottage last night? Why was he following me? Was he monitoring my movements even now? The thought was disquieting.

As soon as the maid let us in, Bridget headed straight for the stairs without a word to anyone.

"Will that be all, miss?" the maid asked.

I realized I'd remained standing in the hallway, lost in thought. "Yes, thank you. Has everyone else retired?"

"Yes'm. Well, g'night," she said, hurrying away.

I went up to our room. Cassie was asleep, dark hair tousled on the pillow, mouth slightly open.

I smothered a yawn of my own as I changed out of my evening frock and into a dark dress that I like to wear for reconnoitering. The fabric is a quiet, lightweight gabardine with deep pockets and a flounce-cut skirt that allows greater freedom of movement. I checked my hiding place for my lockpicks and double-barrel derringer. Strange items to bring on a family visit, to be sure, but I'm accustomed to having them with me. Since my object was the Cliff Walk, I pocketed the gun and left the lockpicks. I wanted to see what the path was like late at night— how navigable it was in the dark, who might be out at such an hour, and how much of the rocky shoreline was visible to the casual observer.

The sharp sea breeze helped revive my flagging energy as I gained the main path. I was glad I'd brought a lantern. Scudding clouds obscured the moon at unpredictable intervals and the few pinpricks of light from the mansions in the distance would not have been enough to guide my steps. Had Eunice carried a lantern with her that fateful night? The newspaper accounts had not included such particulars.

As I crested a rise in the path, much of the bay lay before me, with glimmers of moonlight reflecting upon the water and dark outlines of buildings in the distance. A lone boat bobbed in the water, two men fishing by lantern light. But on the path, no one was about. I continued on.

I'd gone roughly half a mile when I came upon a side path with a decorative wooden sign. *Gull's Bluff.* This was Reg Collinsworth's summer mansion. I hadn't realized they were so close to us, at least via the Cliff Walk. I followed the narrow trail until I had a view of the large house beyond. All the windows were dark. Collinsworth had obviously retired soon after leaving us. I backtracked to the Walk.

After another fifteen minutes on the path, the Forty Steps came into view. Several lanterns glowed along the platform. Even from this distance I could see three men leaning against the railing, chatting and smoking cigarettes. As I approached, the conversation broke off abruptly.

One of the men, tall and wide-shouldered, tipped his cap in

greeting. "Good evening, miss." His voice had the smooth, modulated tones of an educated man.

"Good evening," I answered. "A fine night."

Another man, shorter and of stockier build, ground out his cigarette and rolled down his sleeves. "I should be gettin' back. 'Bye, Joe."

Joe chuckled. "Say hello to that pretty parlor maid who keeps avoiding me—what's her name?"

"Marta." The stocky fellow grinned and wagged a finger. "She's shy. Still, I should be warning her of your smooth-talkin' ways."

The third fellow, quiet up until now and unremarkable except for his unfortunate pockmarked complexion, let out a guffaw. "She'll learn, soon enough."

Joe scowled. "Now, now, none of that talk." He gestured in my direction. "There's a lady present."

The men mumbled apologies as they left. The tall man who'd greeted me remained, looking at me expectantly.

"I'm sorry to have interrupted your conversation," I said.

"No matter. They should have gone already. Mrs. Parker'll be giving them a good talking-to, I expect."

"Parker?"

"Housekeeper to the Collinsworths. She doesn't like them being out so late at night. A bit strict, that one."

"What about you?" I asked.

He took a long drag of his cigarette and flicked it toward the rocks in one fluid motion, born of ease of practice. "My schedule in the evenings is my own." He swept off his cap in a gallant gesture. "Joe Marsh, at your service. I'm Mr. Bancroft's personal secretary."

So that explained his educated accent. He was an employee, but not quite a servant. I could see he took care with his appearance, perhaps to distinguish himself from the domestic servant class. No rolled-up shirtsleeves for this one. His three-piece, gray-check suit had nary a wrinkle, and in the lamp light I caught a glimpse of a gold watch chain dangling from his vest and a ruby-encrusted signet ring upon his little finger.

Something else had caught my attention. The name of his employer—*Bancroft*. My pulse quickened. "I believe I've heard of Mr. Bancroft. Isn't he a scholar?"

"He's many things—notable historian among them. I help him with research, compiling his notes—that sort of thing." He gazed out over the dark expanse of water. "The summers here are the most pleasant part of the job."

"He comes here every summer? I wouldn't have thought a historian need concern himself with Newport high society."

Marsh shook his head. "Bancroft's not one of your ivory-tower academics. He enjoys the summer social doings, and especially likes the seaside. For a man in his eighties he's a vigorous fellow. Boating, fishing...and, bright and early every morning, he walks a few miles."

I had wondered under what pretext I could form an acquaintance with Bancroft. Here was my opportunity. But if I was to catch him on his regular morning walk, I'd better head back.

"Well, I must be going," I said. "It was a pleasure to meet you, Mr. Marsh."

"The pleasure was mine, Miss—why, you haven't told me your name."

"I beg your pardon. I'm Miss Hamilton."

His expression brightened. "Ah, of course! You must be part of the wedding party staying at the Ashton cottage."

"Yes, that's right." Of course he would know that. There was no avoiding the local gossip—and newspaper articles, no doubt—of a fashionable Newport wedding.

I turned to leave before more questions ensued, eager to get to bed so I could intercept George Bancroft in the morning. "Good-bye, Mr. Marsh."

Little did I know at the time, subsequent events the next

morning would occupy me so completely that I quite forgot about Bancroft.

Sunday, June 19th

I woke to the alarm at five in the morning. Though I quickly stifled its tinny ring, Cassie propped up on her elbows and blinked at me in confusion.

"I'm sorry to disturb you, dear, but Mr. Bancroft is an early riser." I buttoned my blouse and reached for my shoes. "I don't want to miss him—"

A shout came from downstairs, followed by the sounds of running feet and the pounding of a bedroom door down the hall.

I stepped into the corridor to see the maid rapping on my mother's door. "Mrs. Hamilton! Come quick! Someone broke into the house!"

In varying states of dishabille, everyone in the household— Papa, Mother, Bridget, Miss Blakely, Cassie and myself— hurried downstairs to join the staff in assessing the situation and figuring out what to do next.

It took me a minute to understand what had first alerted the maid to the burglar. Whoever had broken in had come and gone through the French doors in the dining room. The curtains were a bit disarranged near the door handle, and when the curtains were pulled aside, one could see a pane of glass had been cut out.

I put my hands on my hips and turned to survey the room. The silver candelabras were still here, and the china cabinet looked untouched. "What's been taken?"

Bridget and Miss Blakely exchanged a worried look. "The wedding gifts?" Bridget asked.

"I glanced in the room on our way here," Mother said.

"Items have most certainly been shifted around. We'll have to conduct a thorough inventory."

"I'll help," Miss Blakely offered.

"Thank you, Rebecca," Mother said. "Fetch the gift list, if you please. It's on the writing table in the library." She turned to the housekeeper, who was sifting through her key ring to unlock the china cabinet. "You and your staff must go over everything —the dining room, the kitchen…all of it."

"Yes, ma'am."

Papa, who was accustomed to Mother's take-charge personality, stood by patiently for her to assign him a task. He didn't have long to wait.

"Curtis, you and Cassie help Penelope. I'm sure she knows what to do in the aftermath of such events." She flicked a chilly glance my way. "Prevention would have been more efficacious. I would have thought, with a detective in the house, we would not be subjected to such indignities."

Bridget's surprised expression was quickly replaced with a speculative look that I didn't quite understand.

Papa bristled to my defense. "No one could have anticipated this, Honoria. You said yourself that the cottage was a much *safer* place for the wedding gifts than the Club…." He broke off, eyes widened as he turned back to me. "Wait…a *detective?*"

I crouched down to examine the door more closely and called over my shoulder, "Let us see what's missing, Mother, before we begin recriminations, shall we?"

With a sniff, she left, taking Bridget with her.

"So, how does my daughter come to be mixed up in the detective business?" Papa asked, leaning closer. "Was that your husband's doing?"

"It started out that way," I said, shifting aside the curtain. "I helped Frank with some of his cases, discovered I liked the work and was good at it. Eventually, after we separated, I became a Pinkerton in my own right." I gestured over my shoulder at Cassie. "I need more light. Would you bring over the lamp?"

"No wonder your mother contacted you," Papa said. "But how did she know?"

"Lady Ashton learned of my last case. I understand she's a notorious gossip."

"That she is," he murmured.

Cassie approached with the lamp. "What can you determine, Pen?"

"This man was a professional. The glass was cut with a glazer's knife, you see the clean edge? And there appear to be tape marks—probably to keep it from falling and making noise."

"Oh?" Papa's voice quickened with interest as he hovered even closer. "Fascinating."

Two people breathing down my neck was a bit much. I sat back on my haunches and looked around the floor. "I wonder what he did with the piece of glass. Perhaps it's outside. Papa, would you mind searching for it?"

"Yes, of course," he said, and hurried away.

"Is the piece of glass important?" Cassie asked when he was out of earshot.

I smiled. "Not really."

Her eyes crinkled in merriment. "I see. So, what now?"

"I'm done here. Will you accompany me outside? I want to examine the perimeter next."

"Looking for footprints?" she asked skeptically. "The ground's too dry for that. It hasn't rained since we arrived."

"Any kind of clue, really, to indicate whether he acted alone or had a confederate, how he arrived here, how long he stayed —that sort of thing." I squinted and put a hand to my eyes against the low slant of the morning sun.

"And we need the answer to another question," Cassie said. "Why he picked *this* house, in a town full of extremely wealthy people."

"It could be a common thief looking to steal wedding gifts. Such a one could have read a newspaper account of the upcoming nuptials and learned where we were staying. It's a common tactic among professional thieves to scour the papers for wedding announcements for just such a purpose."

"I see your point. Expensive gifts and personal checks written to the happy couple are out on display or stored somewhere in anticipation of the day."

I hoped it was that simple. I suspected not. Bennett certainly wasn't getting married, and yet his home had been broken into the night before ours. It couldn't be a coincidence.

"You seem rather pensive," she said.

"I haven't had a chance to tell you about other recent developments." I described the events of last night—Collinsworth rising to the bait and racing Bennett on the public road, the accident, the invitation to Bennett's cottage, and my conversation with the newspaper mogul about the burglary at Stone Villa Friday night.

It was a lot to absorb. I gave her time. We walked the grounds, examining the shrub beds beneath the windows and the areas beside the doors, the deep porch, and the front driveway.

Finally, Cassie spoke. "It must be the same man, whether it be the sneak thief from the bank or not. But what is he after?"

We had reached a stand of trees just off to the side of the porch.

"Look!" I pointed. A pile of horse droppings, fairly fresh, lay near the base of a tree amid trampled grass. "A lone man on horseback."

"Well, the horse is obvious," she said, "but how do you know he didn't travel in a conveyance?"

"We're well away from the drive but there are no wheel marks in the grass," I said. "Besides, I didn't hear the rattle of wheels during the night. Did you?"

"No." She pointed. "And he tethered the horse here on the far side of the trees, no doubt to keep anyone from seeing it from the windows."

"You'd make a fine detective, Miss Leigh."

She chuckled. "Now what?"

"I don't think there's any more to be gleaned outdoors. Let's see what progress the others have made. Perhaps we can determine what he was after."

As we turned to go in, Mrs. Mullins, accompanied by her young son Jimmy, came hurrying up the path from the main road. "The stable lad jes' came to fetch me—Lordy! This is—terr'ble." She blew out a breath, pulled out a kerchief, and dabbed at her neck.

Jimmy bounced up and down with excitement, his eyes wide. "Wot's been taken?" he asked, almost gleefully.

"We're still figuring that out, young man," I said mildly.

The cook frowned at her son and gave him a soft cuff on the ear. "Go to the carriage house and make yourself useful, lad."

"Yes'm," he grumbled.

"Sorry, miss," Mrs. Mullins said, watching him go. "He gets carried away. Wot can I do?"

"I'm sure the staff can use your help going through the kitchen. That's your domain more than anyone's."

She flashed me a gratified look. "Know it inside an' out. I'll go look."

CHAPTER 10

*I*n the end only an umbrella was missing. Inconsequential, and—to my contrarian nature— anticlimactic. Such an item was easily borrowed or misplaced rather than stolen. No doubt young Jimmy was disappointed, too.

None of the gifts was missing, though the gift cheques on the display salver had been rifled through, the mantel clock from Mr. Trent had its back pried apart, and the china teapot from Mr. Reeves was found on its side with its lid removed. The intruder had searched the entire lower level, even the kitchen. Mrs. Mullins called me in to see—canisters were pulled out of position, lids returned at awkward angles, even the rubbish bin's contents sifted through.

"What was the thief after? It makes no sense," I said, reaching for the dish of marmalade. Mrs. Mullins had pulled together a late breakfast for us, so Cassie and I, along with Bridget, Miss Blakely, and my parents had gathered around the table in the dining room. "Why rummage around in the kitchen?"

"Maybe he was hungry," Papa joked.

"At least the wedding gifts are all here," Miss Blakely said, "but it's distressing to think of a criminal sneaking in and pawing through everything as we slept." She gave Bridget a sideways glance.

I'd been surreptitiously eyeing my cousin as well. Her pallor and distracted air as she sat, listlessly plucking at her sleeve, bespoke a troubled spirit. No bride should have to deal with such disquieting events.

I turned back to Papa. "Are you going to send for the police?"

He shrugged. "Nothing of value was taken, and I've sent into town for someone to come and mend the door pane."

"That is *not* good enough, Curtis," my mother said. "The burglar could return. How can we stay in this house tonight with any peace of mind?" She turned her hooked nose and steely eyes in my direction. "Well? What are you going to do about it, Penelope?"

I had just drawn breath to assure them of the unlikelihood of the burglar returning—after all, he'd searched exhaustively and had not attained his object as far as we could tell, and surely wouldn't risk discovery by a second attempt—when a male voice broke in.

"Don't worry, Mrs. Hamilton. I have a plan to protect you."

Reg Collinsworth stood in the doorway of dining room. We'd been so absorbed in our discussion no one noticed the maid ushering him in. From the set of his jaw, to his wide, muscled shoulders, to his clenched fists, he looked reassuringly solid, capable, and determined.

Bridget let out a small sob, got up, and ran to him.

He unclenched his hands and opened his arms, holding her close until Papa cleared his throat and he let her go. "I came over as soon as we heard. Grace and I want you to stay at Gull's Bluff until the man is caught. There's plenty of room."

Mother's face took on a pained expression. "Please thank your sister for us, but it wouldn't be at all proper for you two to be under the same roof. You aren't married yet."

Bridget blushed.

"Don't worry, ma'am—I won't be there," Collinsworth said. "I thought I'd keep watch here tonight while you're gone. I can stretch out on the chaise in the parlor. And I'll be bringing my hunting rifle along, just in case."

Papa's eyes lit up. Here, at last, was the prospect of action. And with the added appeal of a hunting rifle, no less. "A fine plan. I'll sit up with you."

"Thank you, sir." Collinsworth said. "If he's foolish enough to return, then we'll have him."

Bridget reached for her fiancé's hand and leaned close. "Thank you, Reg." She dropped her voice, but I still caught the words. "I'm sorry about last night."

He squeezed her hand.

As the breakfast dishes were cleared, the plans were settled for the ladies to direct the packing of necessities and head to the Collinsworth mansion. To my mind it seemed an unnecessary precaution, but there was no budging the others.

The Collinsworth estate, known as Gull's Bluff, was bordered by a brick wall and set well back from the main road. With a brief stop at the ornamental iron gates that creaked as they opened— someone really should attend to that, Mother commented—we proceeded up the long drive to the white-columned front entrance. Servants lined the driveway, ready to assist with our luggage.

"Where's Miss Collinsworth?" Mother asked, as one of the footmen handed her down. I recognized him as the stocky man out who'd idled at the Forty Steps last night.

His glance flicked to me briefly before answering. "She says yu'd want ta settle in yer rooms first."

A woman on the far side of fifty came bustling out just then, her graying hair pulled back in a no-nonsense bun, a large ring of keys dangling from the waist of her spotless blue serge dress. "Forgive me for not coming out sooner, ma'am," she said, addressing my mother. "We've been busy preparing for your arrival. Welcome to Gull's Bluff." She bobbed her head. "I'm Mrs. Parker, the housekeeper. Let me show you to your rooms." She impatiently waved toward the footmen. "Don't dawdle with the cases, lads!"

Inside, she led us up a set of curved marble steps. Sunlight streamed through the stained-glass window along the upper landing, strewing jewel-toned colors at our feet.

"Lovely," Miss Blakely murmured.

"Where's Miss Collinsworth?" Mother asked again, as we followed the housekeeper along the corridor.

"She's waiting for you in the atrium—that's just off the library—whenever you're ready to come down." She opened a series of white-paneled bedroom doors. "Ring if you need anything."

I dawdled behind the others and then took a few wrong turns on my way to the atrium. The Collinsworth mansion was larger than that of the Ashtons'. I wasn't necessarily in a hurry, anyway, and I shamelessly peeked into lower-level rooms along the way.

One of the doors led to what was obviously a music salon, sporting a grand piano, a variety of stringed instruments, music stands, padded chairs, and a thick-piled Turkish rug. I stepped in for a better look and was greeted by an enormous oil portrait of a woman, just past her prime but still striking. I stopped and stared. Who was she? It wasn't Grace. But I'd seen this woman before, long ago.

It took me a moment to realize it was Eunice Collinsworth, née Ivey. In the portrait she was attired in a maroon velvet gown, a rich peacock-adorned fringed shawl sweeping across one porcelain-skin shoulder and artfully brushing the floor. She appeared as prideful, confident, and tightly corseted as I remembered her from the musical entertainments of my youth.

I turned to leave when something else caught my eye. Draped across the piano was the same peacock shawl as in the portrait. A large-brimmed, black-plumed hat, an ivory fan, and a vase of white roses rounded out what was obviously a memorial display of the dead woman's favorite effects.

It somehow felt sacrilegious to stand and stare. I quickly closed the door behind me, nearly bumping into the parlor maid in the process.

"Oh! I beg your pardon, miss," she said, with a quick bob.

She was an exceptionally pretty girl—not surprising, as the parlor maid is usually the first face one sees upon entering a high-society household. She had large, luminous brown eyes, an unblemished complexion, and a curvaceous figure. No doubt the young lads in the neighborhood were smitten.

"Can you please direct me—what's your name?"

"Marta, miss."

"Marta—I seem to have lost my way to the atrium."

She gave a ruby-lipped smile. "I'll take you there, miss."

"We'd been wondering where you were," Bridget said.

"I apologize for the delay." I took a low-slung garden-style seat across from her—how I was going to get myself out of it gracefully was a dilemma for later—and looked around. The stone-floored atrium was more pleasant than a hothouse, though still a bit on the earthy, humid side. Such a space possessed the indoor advantages of controlling the temperature and staying dry in rainy weather while providing pleasant outdoor features, such as the marble fountain that dominated the glass-walled alcove, and an abundance of potted plants that I couldn't pretend to identify.

In one lithe movement, Grace—a low chair was obviously no problem for her—got up and pulled the bell. "I took the liberty of arranging for some light refreshment."

"It's quite kind of you to host us," Mother said.

"Yes," Cassie echoed, "you have a lovely home, Miss Collinsworth. This room, for example, is extraordinary." She nodded toward a sculpted topiary in a large urn. "Your rosemary is as beautiful as it is fragrant. And is that a lemon tree in the corner?"

Grace's eyes lit up. "No lemons as yet, but one hopes. You have a good eye, Miss Leigh." She sighed as her gaze swept the room. "This is my favorite space to read. I'm glad you enjoy it as well."

Over lemonade and raspberry tarts, Grace delicately steered the subject to wedding plans, avoiding mention of the break-in. It would have been natural for the lady to indulge in speculation about the thief as it was our reason for being here, but I was grateful for her restraint. The rest of our party, naturally, was weary of the subject.

"How are the wedding plans coming along, Bridget?" Grace asked.

Bridget set aside her glass. "Extraordinarily well, thanks to Aunt Honoria's hard work." She flashed my mother a grateful glance. Mother returned it with a soft smile and a faint flush of her cheeks.

She really does care about the girl, I thought. It was a surprising side of her to see.

"The gown required some alterations," Bridget went on. "It was my mother's bridal dress. Now that is done. We still have the flowers to settle on, but Lady Ashton kindly offered her extensive rose garden for our use. We also have to confirm the arrangements at the Newport Club."

Mother nodded. "We have an appointment tomorrow with the event planner at the Club to review the menu and settle details as to seating."

Grace gave a wistful sigh. "I do wish you'd have the wedding here."

Bridget's jaw tightened. "I appreciate the offer, Grace, but the disruption to your home would be too great. We're expecting nearly two hundred guests."

"This"—Grace waved a hand in an encompassing gesture —"will be *your* home, dear. And what a special place it is. My father had this atrium built when I was a child, to allow us to enjoy the benefits of nature no matter the weather." Her voice softened. "There are many good memories here. You and Reg will create even more in the years to come."

Out of the corner of my eye I noticed Bridget bring her napkin to her lips to hide a grimace.

Mother leaned forward. "I know you live here year 'round, Grace, but that won't be the case for your brother and Bridget. At most they would summer here."

Rebecca Blakely clucked in sympathy. "I can understand you wanting the company, Miss Collinsworth. It's such a large place to live alone."

"Once Reg is married I won't be staying here in the main house," Grace said. "Far be it for me to intrude upon newlyweds. There's a smaller house upon the grounds that's quite comfortable. Reg had it built for me when he married Eunice."

"A dower house of sorts?" I asked.

Grace made a face. "I'm hardly a dowager, Pen. Though I suppose it serves the same purpose."

A short silence followed. Bridget cleared her throat. "Why don't you come with us to the Club tomorrow, Grace? I could use your advice as to menu preferences. I know no one from Reg's side of the family besides you, and certainly nothing of what anyone likes."

Grace brightened. Perhaps she'd been feeling left out of the wedding plans.

"I thought we'd find you here," a male voice chimed in. Reg Collinsworth walked in, flanked by Maxwell Trent and Donald Reeves.

Reg kissed his sister on the top of her head. "Sharing your favorite spot with our guests, I see. And was that wedding talk I heard?" His mischievous eyes met Bridget's from across the room.

"Of course it is," Bridget said, "as it's invariably up to the ladies to handle such preparations."

Collinsworth put a hand to his chest in mock astonishment. "Up to the ladies? I don't know what you're talking about, my dear. After all, I had to buy the ring."

Trent chortled as he and Reeves brought in seats from the library. Collinsworth, of course, placed his chair as close to Bridget's as possible, and Miss Blakely blushed as Trent pulled over an ottoman to sit at her feet. That left poor Reeves with a choice of spinsters and one formidable matron. The plucky fellow chose the latter. Mother shifted to make room.

"We're joining Reg in setting his trap tonight," Reeves said, rubbing his hands in glee. "Should be fun!"

Mother blinked. "I beg your pardon?"

"I told Trent and Reeves here about our plan to keep watch at The Cedars tonight and catch the burglar," Collinsworth said. "They've offered to keep us company."

Trent gave an enthusiastic nod, smoothing away a lock of brown hair from his forehead in an endearing little-boy gesture.

Miss Blakely turned her unladylike squeal into a more decorous exclamation. "Oh! Are you sure that's quite safe?" She gazed at Trent with worried blue eyes.

Trent grinned. "Don't you worry, Miss Blakely, we'll be well armed. We can handle him."

I hid a snicker behind my napkin. Collinsworth's simple plan to sit up all night with only a hunting rifle and Papa to keep him company had become a veritable gentlemen's smoker. I doubted any covert vigil-keeping would take place tonight. Not that it mattered. The burglar was unlikely to return.

CHAPTER 11

$\mathcal{I}$'d barely grown accustomed to sleeping at the Ashton cottage when we'd relocated to Gull's Bluff, so it was no surprise that sleep eluded me much of the night. Thoughts of Eunice Collinsworth turned in my mind, no doubt prompted by the sight of her portrait and personal items. How was I to get answers about her death? The events of this morning had thwarted my efforts to speak with Bancroft.

Finally tired of staring at the ceiling, I got up, shook out my twisted nightgown, and stepped to the balcony for some air.

I smelled the rain before I saw it, so I opened the balcony door only enough to look out at the swaying pines that flanked the back end of the property. If it continued in earnest, encountering Bancroft on the Cliff Walk in the morning wouldn't be feasible.

Well then, my next step would be to call upon the reporter who wrote the articles about Eunice's death. Tomorrow was… Monday? Perfect. The newspaper offices would be open.

A bit of movement on the grounds below caught my dark-adjusted eyes. A female in a dark dress, shawl over her head against the rain, was hurrying toward the back door directly below into the kitchen. Everyone had retired long ago.

Was it the housekeeper? Or Marta, sneaking off to meet a young man? I craned my neck for a better look, but she was gone.

Monday, June 20th

I had the breakfast room to myself and was just finishing when Bridget came down. Her shadowed eyes, pale cheeks, and stifled yawns hinted at a night as restless as my own.

"'Morning, Pen." She reached for a teacup. "Any word from your father or Reg?"

"Both, actually. Mrs. Mullins's youngster, Jimmy, stopped by a little while ago with letters. Here's yours." I passed her an envelope. "Papa said last night was uneventful."

"Hardly surprising." Bridget's lips twitched as she scanned her note. "Apparently Trent and Reeves were bored by nine o'clock and were none too quiet the remainder of the night."

I chuckled. "Four men keeping watch together is not conducive to stealth. Then there was the miserable rain last night to deter a would-be intruder. *If* he'd planned to return at all, which I've doubted all along."

She nodded absently, eyes straying back to the note in her hand. "I hope this means we can return today."

"You aren't comfortable here?"

"Grace is a wonderful hostess, of course. But to stay in the house where Reg's first wife lived...have you seen the music salon?"

I winced. "I have. I'm surprised your fiancé would keep such memorabilia on display." He didn't strike me as the sentimental sort.

"It's not his fault, really. The portrait has been hanging there since they first married. But the rest of it—the hat, the fan, the shawl, the vase of fresh flowers—that's all the housekeeper's doing. She was apparently quite fond of Eunice. She'd been in her service for a long while, and came here with her mistress after the marriage. Grace and Reg decided to avoid offending her and left it alone."

"Good housekeepers are hard to find, I suppose, but it seems extraordinary lengths to go to," I said.

"Neither of them goes into the salon very often," Bridget said.

"Well, you have the right to redecorate the place as you like when you take possession of it—no matter how the housekeeper feels about it."

Bridget shook her head vehemently. "I've already told Reg I cannot live here after we're married—not even as a summer residence. I would prefer to summer in the Hamptons and be out of Newport completely, but his yachting club is here."

"What will you do, then?"

"He's agreed to sell this property and buy us another nearby. And arrange something for Grace, too, of course," she added quickly.

I thought back to Grace's look of contentment in the atrium. "I'm assuming she hasn't been told of the plan?"

Bridget hesitated. "He's put off telling her. She loves it here." She shivered. "As for me, I want to get as far from this house as possible."

"Why? Eunice didn't die here."

She bit her lip at my blunt remark.

There was never going to be a better occasion to discuss the matter. We may as well do it now. "Bridget, what has Reg told you about his wife's death?"

She didn't look at me, instead fiddling with the napkin in her lap. "Only what everyone else knows—that she was out on the Cliff Walk, fell, and died."

"Does he know why she was out on the path so late at night?"

"He's as surprised by that as anyone. His best guess is that she was upset and took a walk."

"Upset by what?"

"They had quarreled that day. He'd left in a huff."

"Do you know the reason for the quarrel?"

"He didn't want to discuss it. I didn't press. I know he feels guilty about leaving her alone after what then happened."

"Are you sure that's all he feels guilty about?" I asked.

Her hands stilled. She gave me a sharp look. "I know about the note sent to Aunt Honoria."

"Oh? You never said anything."

"Her little secrets seem terribly important to her."

Perceptive girl. "You haven't said anything to your fiancé, I hope?"

"No." She gave a shaky laugh. "How would one go about doing that?"

"True enough. Don't be angry with Mother. She was trying to protect you." Here was a first—me making excuses for my mother.

"I'm no shrinking violet, Pen." She scowled. "What I find more distressing is that she took it seriously enough to ask you to investigate my husband-to-be, and you're going along with it. Reg did not kill his wife, and I will never believe otherwise." She stood. "Excuse me."

Cassie was walking into the breakfast room as Bridget pushed past her.

Cassie raised a dark eyebrow at her departing back, then looked at me. "Bridal nerves? Or was it something you said?"

"What do you think?" I said testily. "The conversation turned to Eunice Collinsworth. She knows about the note, by the way—and the fact that Mother asked me to look into it." And she'd learned yesterday morning I was a detective. She must have put it all together then.

Cassie was helping herself from the toast rack. She turned, tongs still in hand. "She knows? Oh, dear. How incredibly awkward. Does Collinsworth know, too?"

"She says not, but it's only a matter of time, I'm sure—" I

broke off as Mother and Grace walked into the breakfast room next.

"Good morning, Miss Hamilton," Grace said, smothering a yawn.

Did no one sleep well in this house?

"Good morning, Miss Collinsworth. 'Morning, Mother."

My mother reached for a plate. "Good morning, Penelope. You're up early. Any word?"

I tapped Papa's note. "No sign of an intruder last night. Papa believes there's nothing further to be concerned about."

Grace exhaled. "That's a relief."

"Um, Miss Collinsworth," Cassie called from the buffet table, her tone sheepish, "can you ring for a footman? I'm afraid I'm stuck." She gestured to her bracelet, caught in an ornately curved bracket of the chafing tray.

"Oh, goodness!" Grace exclaimed.

"I don't want to damage anything. If I could just—oh!" Cassie held up her freed wrist in delight as Grace mercilessly snapped off the wire. "You didn't have to break it. I'm sorry."

"Nonsense." Grace shrugged. "It's a hideous dish, anyway."

She was right about that. Mother's lips twitched.

I set aside my napkin. "I must be going. I have an errand in town." I turned to Grace. "Thank you for your hospitality."

She clasped my hand. "My pleasure."

"Pen," Cassie asked, "will you be joining us at the Newport Club today to help Bridget review the menu?"

I doubted my contributions would be of much help, but I wanted to make it up to my cousin for angering her. "Of course. What time?"

"We meet with the caterer at two o'clock," Mother said.

"Fine. I should be back before then."

During the short carriage ride to the Swinburne Building off of Thames Street, which housed the *Newport Daily News*, I mentally rehearsed the tale I'd concocted to explain my interest in Mrs. Collinsworth's death. Thankfully, the rain had stopped by the time we arrived. I picked my way carefully around the puddles to reach the door.

A man sitting at the lobby desk looked up. "Yes, miss, what can I do for you?"

"Actually, it's *Mrs.*," I said. "Mrs. Pratt, with the *Chicago Ladies' Journal*. I wish to speak with one of your reporters...a Mr. Tucker Gannon. Is he available?"

He scratched his head as he looked me over. Perhaps not many lady journalists cross his path. "Got a card I can give him, ma'am?"

I made a show of digging into my reticule, pulling out a pencil and the imposing-looking stenography pad I'd liberated from Collinsworth's study to give myself an official air. I hoped he wouldn't miss a few pages when I was done with it. "Hmm, I don't see them. In my hurry, I must have left the cards in my luggage."

"I see. Well, Mr. Gannon is a busy man, you know"—

—"I shan't keep him long, I promise," I interrupted, smiling sweetly. "I'm working on a background piece for my article. I have only a few questions."

The man sighed, reached for a scrap of paper, and began scribbling. "Mrs. Pratt, you say? And what publication do you work for?"

"The *Ladies' Journal*."

"All right, then. Wait here and I'll check."

I'd only gotten halfway through counting the divots in the parquet flooring when he returned. "This way."

He led me upstairs and through a maze of desks and file cabinets. The air was thick with the musty smell of damp windowsills, old ink, and cheap paper. I put a gloved finger under my nose to stifle a sneeze. Finally we reached a corner space beside a tall window. "Mr. Gannon? Mrs. Pratt, sir." With one last glance of curiosity in my direction, he left us.

Gannon's desk was littered with sliding stacks of papers atop a stained desk blotter. A chipped mug, crammed with pencils, perched upon the tallest pile.

The man was as unkempt as his desk, attired in a wrinkled suit, loosened tie, and pushed-up shirtsleeves. His jacket lay huddled upon a nearby stool.

He grabbed the jacket and tossed it on the floor in the corner. "Mrs. Pratt, please sit. What can I do for you?"

I resisted the urge to swipe the seat with my handkerchief before settling in. "I'm writing a background piece for our Society page, about the principals involved in the Sinclair-Collinsworth wedding. It will run the day before the wedding, in anticipation of the event itself. Our readership is quite interested in the lives of high society. I've already spoken at length with Miss Sinclair and her family. However, my information about Mr. Collinsworth is incomplete."

Gannon leaned back in his chair and clasped his hands over his lumpy middle. "Why me, ma'am? I'm not a society columnist. What would I know about the Collinsworths?"

I affected surprise. "I read several articles you wrote about the Collinsworth tragedy two summers ago. I assumed, in the process of interviewing them during their time of grief, you had come to know the family well."

He sighed. "Grief either loosens tongues or constricts them. That family was extremely close-mouthed."

I flipped open my notepad. "The angle I'm taking with my article is that of a well-deserved happy ending—a lonely, grieving widower finding joy at last. One must at least touch upon the sad part of the tale in order to get to the happy outcome."

He let out a bark of laughter. "Reg Collinsworth, lonely? Hardly."

"Oh? He kept company with the ladies after his wife's death?"

"Don't go writing that down," he growled. "That wouldn't fit at all with your 'happy ending'."

"Point taken. Well then, about Mrs. Collinsworth's death—what can you tell me? I understand she fell from a seaside path to the rocks and water below. What time did it happen?"

He shrugged. "No one knows exactly. She dismissed her personal maid at midnight. No one saw her alive after that. The doctor said she'd been dead several hours before she was found."

"And she was found—when?"

He chewed on the end of his pencil as he thought. "Half-past five. Fellow named Bancroft found her."

I scribbled a note in my pad. "George Bancroft, is that correct? Where exactly was her husband?"

"Visiting a friend in Portsmouth. That fellow Trent—you know, Collinsworth's best man—has a brownstone there. An excellent tie-in for your article—the friend who was there in both sorrow and joy."

I firmly suppressed a smile as I made a point of writing it down. The man had a flair for melodrama. "Yes, a noteworthy connection." In more ways than one. "You reported in your follow-up article that, according to the coroner, Mrs. Collinsworth didn't drown. How did he determine that? She was found in the water, correct?"

Gannon grimaced. "There was no fluid in her lungs. Naturally, I couldn't include such grisly detail. This is a respectable paper—you'll find none of that sensational, yellow journalism here."

"Naturally."

"The entire affair seemed so...preventable. Such a tragedy. Had Collinsworth been home, I doubt the wife would have gone out on the Cliff Walk alone at that hour."

"Why *was* she out so late?"

He narrowed his eyes. "How is that pertinent to your story, Mrs. Pratt?"

I sniffed in mild disdain. "I take it you have little experience with an all-female readership. The ladies who peruse our magazine are fascinated by the lives of the wealthy and fashionable, including details you gentlemen might consider trivial."

"*Hmph.* I suppose. There's not much about the lady's motives to fascinate your readers, however. She obviously wanted some air."

"Was she in the habit of strolling along the Cliff Walk for such a purpose?"

"I asked that question at the time. By all accounts, Mrs. Collinsworth rarely visited the Walk. Didn't even bring a lantern with her, on a night when the moon had clouded over. Little wonder she lost her footing."

I couldn't quite tell, but he may have muttered *Lord save us from impulsive females.* I chose to ignore it as I stood. "Thank you, sir. I appreciate your time."

He gave a curt nod. "At least your ladies will get their happy ending."

I sincerely hoped so.

I stepped out to the sidewalk. The fog was lifting as the sun struggled to break through the clouds. Where to next? It seemed I could go no further in investigating Eunice Collinsworth's death until I spoke to Bancroft. I was still committed to making this as discreet an inquiry as possible, so my original plan to casually encounter him on the Cliff Walk first thing in the morning remained my best option. I would have to try again tomorrow. In the meantime, a talk with Gordon Bennett might be a good use of my time. He didn't know about our break-in Sunday morning. Perhaps he'd made progress on his own.

Since I was already close to the wharf, I decided to see if his yacht was docked. I crossed Thames Street in that direction.

It didn't take long before I had the distinct impression I was being followed. I stepped away from the foot traffic of the sidewalk toward an alley, where I pulled out my compact mirror and adjusted my hat. It took a bit of discreet angling, but I managed to see him in the small oval. It was the blond man once again. He stood in front of a shop window at the corner, idly scratching his head beneath his cap as he made a show of contemplating the merchandise. I waited, tucking invisible wisps of hair, until I saw a group of people approach, effectively blocking me from his view.

Now was my chance.

I scooted down the alley and into the gloom, dodging rubbish bins and coal chutes. Over the sound of my heartbeat thudding in my ears, I heard rapid footsteps turn into the alley. I hitched up my skirts and quietly climbed atop a damp tarpaulin-covered stack of crates. I'd just settled the cover over me— suppressing a shiver as a trickle of leftover rainwater rolled down my neck—when I heard the footsteps coming closer.

I kept my breaths shallow as I strained to listen. The footsteps passed my hiding spot, hesitated, then returned. He was just below me now, searching among the bins and crates littering the alley. The faint rattle of a latch reached my ears. He was testing rear doors to the shops that opened onto the alley, in case I'd escaped that way.

But escape wasn't my intention. I was tired of being the prey, and planned to turn hunter in this little chase.

CHAPTER 12

*M*y foot was just starting to cramp in my crouched
position when I heard him move toward the far
end of the alley, his steps fading. I quietly slipped out from
under the tarp, jumped down from the crates—much to the
speechless astonishment of a shopkeeper's delivery boy who'd
just stepped outside—and quickly put my clothing to rights
before trailing after the man.

He was in no hurry now, which didn't surprise me. After all,
even though he'd lost sight of me, he knew where I was staying.
He stopped to buy a paper from a newsie at the corner and
headed for the wharf. I hung back, then found a safer vantage
point behind a large pillar as he turned toward a line of benches
beside the water, placed there so onlookers can admire the
yachts that come in.

I recognized the steam yacht pulling into a slip, though only
by name—the *Namouna*. It was Bennett's vessel, and certainly an
impressive sight. It looked to be over two hundred feet long, with
three iron masts, flying the American flag as well as what looked
to be Bennett's own colors. The *Namouna*'s main deck swarmed
with activity as a dozen men variously worked to disassemble
deck awnings, stack crates, and throw ropes to waiting hands to

settle her into her moorings. There was no sign of Bennett himself.

I shifted my attention back to my would-be pursuer. Instead of reading his newspaper, he'd pulled out a pencil and a slim, bound book from his jacket pocket and began to write.

He took a long time over his writing, head bent over the pages, shoulders tight in concentration.

Associations are funny things—a look, a scent, a gesture, a trick of the light—who's to say how such connections are forged in the human mind? All I knew was the sight brought back memories of my estranged Pinkerton husband, hunched over his logbook as he recorded the status of a case in progress. There seemed to be a great deal about this trip, in fact, that had me involuntarily thinking of Frank.

But in this instance I welcomed it, because now I had a good idea of who this stranger might be. There was only one way to know for sure.

Eventually, the man stood, stretched, tucked away both book and newspaper, and made his way toward Thames Street. I suspected he was going to check the alley one more time, perhaps interview the shopkeepers along the stretch to see if any had noticed a tall, slim woman with hair as blond as his own. That's what I would have done.

I crossed the street and caught up to him just as he turned into the alley. "Why, Cousin Charles, what a surprise to see you here!" I clasped his arm before he had a chance to react. With my other hand, I reached into his right-hand pocket for the gun I was sure he had there. I withdrew it in one quick, fluid motion and held it out of sight within the folds of my skirt. "Let us have a conversation and catch up. So much has happened since we last spoke, wouldn't you agree?"

The man gaped up at me—I had the advantage of height as well as surprise—as I steered him toward the shadowed side of the alley. I prodded him toward a sack of potatoes that leaned against a discarded wagon wheel. "Sit down. We have much to discuss."

He raised his hands in a gesture of innocence as he reluctantly complied. "Look, lady, I don't know who you are or what you want, but if this is some sort of prank, I have no time for it. Give me my gun and I'll go."

I glanced down at his revolver, a common five-shot, top-break variety. It was a good bit larger than my own derringer, but men have the pockets for a bigger weapon—women, sadly, do not. "You'll get it back after you've answered my questions."

He made a move as if to get up.

I raised the gun and cocked it. "Don't try it," I said calmly. "I am perfectly capable of shooting you."

He eyed me as I kept the gun steady, pointed at his heart. "I believe it." He eased himself back to the seated position.

"That's better." I warily lowered the weapon. "Who hired you to follow me?"

"Follow you?" he echoed. "What do you mean?"

"Don't play the innocent. You're a private detective. I want to know what sort of case is important enough to drive you to attempted robbery and two break-ins, along with following my movements these past few days."

The parade of conflicting expressions on the man's face was a sight to behold—wariness, shock, and grudging admiration each fought for residence there. Finally, what took their place was a speculative expression as he regarded me.

"I seem to have underestimated you, Miss Hamilton. You're more than you appear to be—tell me, what case are *you* working on?"

I suppose it was inevitable that he would have guessed. It's not every day that a lady accosts you in an alley with your own gun.

When I didn't reply, he added, "We'd heard William Pinkerton had hired a woman operative a couple of years ago. Might that be you?"

I tipped my head with a sigh.

"That explains a few things," he murmured to himself, then rose—carefully, showing me his hands, keeping his distance. "Very well, Miss Hamilton, I suppose you are entitled to an explanation, though I'm counting upon your discretion." He turned his head to survey the alley. "Shall we talk somewhere more...congenial? There's a sandwich shop around the corner."

If someone had told me I'd be drinking tea while seated across from the man who I'd chased out of a bank, I would have questioned such a one's sanity.

Even so, his gun remained in my reticule.

He waited until our server had left us. "I'm sorry for the trouble. I wasn't sure of your involvement in this matter. At first, it appeared you might be in league with Tompkins when you thwarted me at the bank—"

"You gave every appearance of being a sneak thief," I interrupted. "Who would fail to intervene, under the circumstances?"

He snorted. "Few ladies pay such close attention much less give chase down the block. I was fortunate to have a waiting conveyance, or you might have caught me then."

"What did you want from Mr. Bennett's valet?" I asked. "Not his money, I presume."

He shook his head. "Coffee."

I realized my mouth had dropped open. I shut it. "Before we go any further, I want to see your identification."

He hesitated, then passed it over.

Johnston Shaw, private investigator
Gold Star Investigations
New York / Boston / Hartford

I handed it back. "Thank you."

"And yours, Miss Hamilton?" he asked, tucking away the billfold. "Since we're exercising caution here."

I obliged, and he gave it a good look before returning it. "Well then, we understand each other."

"I understand very little, Mr. Shaw. What has Tompkins done? And what does coffee have to do with it?"

He sat back and folded his arms. "What happened to the tin? I learned Bennett gave it to you, but it was nowhere to be found when I searched your cottage."

The men with whom I'd lately conversed had an annoying habit of ignoring my questions and countering with their own. I hoped it wouldn't become a trend. "I don't know, precisely. Our cook transferred the grounds to a separate container. Probably disposed of the tin." I wasn't about to tell him that Cassie had the receptacle until Shaw told me more. I frowned. *Did* Cassie get the tin back after it was cleaned? In the hubbub of the past few days, I couldn't remember.

"It wasn't in the rubbish bin," he said. "I looked."

"What's so special about a coffee tin? And what is Tompkins's role? Explain."

"First, I want your word that you won't share this with anyone. If it reached the wrong people, it would undo weeks of painstaking work."

"Of course."

He leaned closer. "Tompkins is a check forger. A very good one, in fact."

I sucked in a breath. "You have proof of this?"

"Yes."

"Then why not arrest him?"

"He's part of a bigger operation. We want to catch the entire ring. This particular scheme targets wealthy families in the area. Canceled checks are stolen, forged, and then cashed at an out-of-town bank."

"Really? How do they get hold of the canceled checks in the first place?"

"Right out of the owner's study. Servants, family, and even some visitors have that sort of access, unless the owner is diligent about keeping the room locked. Once the check is taken it's passed along to Tompkins to copy from. But the real brilliance of the operation—and why it took a while to figure out—is the stolen checks are returned to their original places before the owners are ever the wiser."

"Ingenious, but risky," I said. "The thief has to get into the owner's study twice. Then there is the issue of transporting the original checks to be restored and the forged ones to be cashed. I'm assuming a confederate presents the spurious check to the bank, not Tompkins."

"That's right. The workings are fairly compartmentalized, from the person who steals the canceled check and later returns it, to Tompkins, and to the check-casher. People at one end or the other don't necessarily know each other. It's the intermediary who's key to the whole scheme, and who I believe orchestrated it to begin with."

"And you know who that is?"

"I've had some people under surveillance besides Tompkins, but I suspect the tin would supply me with the proof I need."

"What people?" I asked.

His expression took on a shuttered look. "I need to keep that to myself for now."

"So that's why you searched the kitchen." I closed my eyes to better recall the coffee container. It was unremarkable—square, metal, sized to hold a pound of ground coffee…ah, but…it was a local, custom blend, with a blue-speckled paper label wrapped around its girth. Mass-produced goods had their labels simply painted on. "You believe the checks are hidden under the label."

"I do."

"Why would the criminals go to such lengths when a simple envelope would suffice? Or a book, if one wanted to be more devious?"

"Papers can fall out of a book, and envelopes pass through too many hands to be secure—the postman, the footman who sorts through the mail—"

"The person in question keeps servants?" I asked incredulously. "We're talking about a person of means, not a petty
criminal?"

"I really shouldn't say any more on the subject."

"Did you take an umbrella from our cottage?" I asked.

He nodded. "Tompkins was handed the coffee tin *and* an
umbrella on his stop before the bank. Since I couldn't find the
tin—I'd spent too long at the cottage as it was, and I heard
someone in the house moving about—I grabbed the umbrella
on my way out. I thought Tompkins may have passed it on to
you." He made a face. "Nothing there."

"That wasn't his umbrella to begin with, but I grant you
they all tend to look alike. Why did you search among the
wedding gifts?"

He'd obviously wearied of my questions by that point, as a
look of irritation crossed his face. "I was merely being
thorough."

"Did you find anything at Bennett's place? He said nothing
was taken."

"Nothing that revealed anything new," Shaw said. "Now, it's
your turn—what case are you working on? I find it hard to
believe you're here for a family wedding."

"Why not?" I stalled, not sure how much to tell him. "I'm
quite fond of my cousin."

Then I had an idea. Perhaps Shaw could be of use to me. I
waited until the busboy had finished collecting our dishes and
left us. "There *is* a personal matter that requires my attention.
You might be able to help. How familiar are you with the local
history? Do you live hereabouts?"

"I'm from Middletown, the next township north of here. Far
enough away that I'm not recognized in Newport, but I get most
of the gossip. What do you want to know?"

I explained the anonymous warning note and the mysterious
circumstances of Eunice Collinsworth's death.

He made a face. "I heard about the lady, of course, but foul play wasn't suspected."

"So say the newspaper accounts."

"*Ah*, that was why you were at the Swinburne building this morning. You must have been checking with the reporter. Learn anything?"

"Not much, though the time frame of her death is a bit more solid now. I have another person to talk to."

"What do you want from me, then?"

"Can you look into the finances of Reginald Collinsworth? Income, assets, spending habits. I especially want to know how well off he was before marrying Eunice, and if there were any financial irregularities during the time of their marriage."

He quirked a sandy-blond eyebrow. "You mean the kind of irregularities that only a large influx of money would solve? Money the wife had control over during the marriage but might have been reluctant to part with?"

He was quick.

"Exactly."

"I already have a case. What's in it for me?"

"Extra money, for one." I'd happily turn over whatever Mother paid me for the successful resolution of the matter, though of course she'd be furious if she knew I was confiding in a stranger about a private family affair. I was crossing a very big line in enlisting Shaw's help. "That's in addition to returning your gun, helping in the search for the coffee tin, and most of all"—I narrowed my eyes in his direction—"my keeping quiet about what you told me, including how I managed to trap you to get it."

It was the last part that did it.

Shaw sat back with a faint hiss. He wouldn't dare let it be known a woman had bested him, even if she was a Pinkerton.

"All right," he growled.

"We have to make progress quickly," I said. "She's to marry Collinsworth in five-days' time."

"You don't ask much, do you?" He pursed his lips as he thought. "I do have a working acquaintance with an investment broker who summers here. He knows everybody who's anybody. I'll try him first."

"Good. Where are you staying?"

He shook his head. "Don't come to me. I'll send word when I have something. Tomorrow, I expect."

"What if I find the tin in the meantime? I have an idea of where to look. You'll want to know right away, I assume."

He considered that a moment. "All right, I see your point. I'm at Ocean House, under the name Johnny Sharpe. But for heaven's sake, don't inquire for me there. Send a note if you find the tin."

I got up from my chair. "Provided our glass door panes remain intact, I won't have to come looking for you."

He held up a hand in a mock pledge. "No more break-ins. Promise."

"Oh, and one more thing," I said, as he followed me out of the shop, "I assume you keep a written account of your case-work. I would appreciate it if any reference to me in your notes is not identifiable. This needs to be a discreet inquiry."

"Done."

The sun was drying up the last of the puddles along the sidewalk and affording us a clear view of the wharf across the street. I could even make out the faces of people aboard the *Namouna* from here. Gordon Bennett was above deck now, attired in a crisp-white three-piece suit and a jaunty straw boater. He passed a briefcase over to...yes, there stood his valet, Tompkins. I grimaced. Verbally sparring with the newspaper mogul so as not to divulge his valet's nefarious side activities was an exhausting prospect. I'd have to keep my distance from those two.

Shaw cleared his throat and murmured, "You forgot some-thing, Miss Hamilton. My gun?"

"Oh. Yes, of course." I plucked it from my reticule, turning the handle toward his waiting grasp. "My apologies, Mr. Shaw. Tomorrow, then?"

He tipped his cap and walked away.

I smiled to myself as I glanced once again across the wharf at the *Namouna*.

And locked eyes with James Gordon Bennett. Even from this distance, I could see his look was thunderous.

CHAPTER 13

$\mathcal{M}$y first order of business when I returned to the Ashton cottage was to lay my hands on the coffee container. I hurried to our room, where Cassie was unpacking.

"I declined the maid's offer to unpack your bag," she said. "I know you like to do it yourself. How was your excursion? Did you learn anything?"

"Not nearly enough. Tell me, did Mrs. Mullins ever give you the coffee tin back?"

She frowned. "I'd forgotten about that. No."

I bit my lip. This wasn't going to be as straightforward as I'd hoped. "I see. I'll go ask."

Cassie waved a dismissive hand. "Never mind. I don't want to bother her."

"It can't hurt to check. She may have set it aside somewhere." Though where that might be when Shaw had searched the entire ground floor, I couldn't imagine.

The cook stood at the stove, stirring one pot while adding chopped vegetables to another. The steam was curling her red hair in tendrils along her forehead, which she swiped at impatiently whenever a hand was free.

"Excuse me—Mrs. Mullins?"

She whipped around, face creased in annoyance.

"I'm sorry to disturb you, but"—

"Jus' a minute, miss...Jimmy!" she called, rummaging in an apron pocket.

The boy looked up from the celery he'd been chopping. "Yes, Ma?" He glanced over at me in recognition. "Oh. Hullo."

Mrs. Mullins pulled out a small pair of shears. "I need more rosemary. Snip six nice long stalks for me, there's a good boy. But don't dawdle outside on your way back, ya hear?"

He grinned. "Yes'm."

"Wot can I do for ya, miss?" she asked, as the screen door slammed behind him.

"You remember the coffee we brought you a few days ago? My friend Cassie had asked to keep the container. Do you know where it is?"

She made a grumbling noise in the back of her throat as she turned again to the stove. "I think it got thrown out in the rubbish. We was real busy and I forgot. Sorry 'bout that."

I crossed the room and lifted the lid of the kitchen pail. "In here?"

She glanced over her shoulder. "Nah. That gets emptied daily into a larger receptacle outside. But I'm sure it's been carted away by now. The man comes on Monday mornings."

"Oh."

She gave me a sharp look. "Why's that partic'lar tin so special? Can't the young lady use something else?"

"Yes, of course. I'll let you get back to your work."

Just to be sure, I went around to the back of the property where the rubbish was kept for the garbage collector. Lifting the hatch and holding my nose, I peeked inside. Empty. No chance of finding it now.

The rest of the afternoon produced an all-too-familiar restlessness as I awaited word from Shaw. Leery of running into Bennett at his own club and having to dodge his questions, I pleaded a headache and stayed home while the ladies went to the Newport Club to finalize wedding plans.

The solitude was welcome. I decided to stroll the Cliff Walk and try to sort out the bits I'd gleaned from Bridget and the newspaper reporter. Almost without thinking, my steps turned south, toward Bancroft's Rosecliff estate.

What did I know so far? Reg Collinsworth and his wife had quarreled that day. Then he'd headed for Portsmouth…to *Trent's* lodgings in town. According to both men, he'd stayed the night.

What if Trent had been lying for his friend? Certainly the authorities had located Collinsworth there when they broke the news to him the following day. However, he could have been in Newport the night before. It was only a few hours away by carriage. He could have killed his wife and driven directly to Portsmouth, well before his wife's body was discovered. As long as he avoided being seen in Newport and Trent backed up his story, it was a solid alibi.

There was a complication to that, of course. Both Bridget and the reporter had said Mrs. Collinsworth didn't regularly visit the Walk. Collinsworth would have had to lure her to that spot on some pretext. I scowled. In the middle of the night? It seemed improbable.

The breeze had picked up and I was just about to turn back on the path when I spotted a trim-built, white-bearded man heading briskly in my direction. My heart beat faster.

Could it be Bancroft?

The man tipped his twill cap as he approached. "Afternoon, miss."

"Good afternoon." I stopped. "Pardon my presumption, but I'm a visitor to the area. How much farther does this path progress? Is there a loop or do I need to retrace my steps?"

"There's no loop, you'll have to double-back eventually. Where are you staying, Miss—?"

"Hamilton. Penelope Hamilton." I extended a hand, which he bowed over gallantly. "We're at the Ashton cottage. My cousin is to be married on Saturday."

His white, shaggy brows went up in recognition. "Ah, I heard about that. My felicitations to the young lady. She's marrying Collinsworth, I believe. Glad to hear the fellow is finding some happiness."

"You know, then, about the first Mrs. Collinsworth's passing?" I inquired. "You must be a local."

"In a manner of speaking." He swept the cap off his head. "George Bancroft, at your service." He pointed vaguely in the southerly direction from which he'd come. "Rosecliff is my summer home."

"I believe I met your secretary the other evening, farther along the Walk. Mr. Marsh."

Bancroft grunted. "I pay him entirely too much for all the leisure time he takes in the late evenings, strolling along the Walk and fraternizing with the servants at the Forty Steps. But he's an excellent researcher. I do hope he didn't speak to you out of turn. Likes to chat with the fairer sex overmuch."

Recalling Marsh's suave manner and the less-than-subtle remarks of his fellows, I doubted his time with the ladies was confined to mere conversation. "Never fear, he was personable without being impertinent. Our conversation did turn to the sad topic of Eunice Collinsworth's death. He said you were the one who found her that morning."

"Damn and blast, he talks too much," Bancroft muttered under his breath, jamming his cap back on his head.

I pretended not to hear. "What a shock that must have been. Is it true that no one knows why she'd gone to the Walk so late that night—and without a lantern?"

He didn't answer right away. He stood, hands in his pockets, gazing at the shoreline below.

"Sir?" I prompted. "Do you know why she would've been

out on the Walk at that hour?" A thought struck me. "Perhaps she was meeting someone?"

"Possibly," he murmured. "There was that one time when I wondered, but...*him*? No, no, that's absurd...."

"What do you mean?" I asked.

He roused himself. "*Hmm*? Nothing. I'm afraid my mind wandered. I was thinking of something else. I beg your pardon —I must be going. A pleasure to meet you, Miss Hamilton."

I was eager to share with Cassie what I'd learned from Bancroft, but it turned out my solitude was to be extended for a while longer. Mother sent a note to explain that Grace Collinsworth had invited the ladies back to Gull Bluff for dinner and cards. I was invited to join them, but a tray in my room and retiring early seemed more appealing than more wedding talk.

Tuesday, June 21st

The French doors of the dining room were already open to catch the breeze when I came down the next morning. Cassie was the only one at breakfast.

"'Morning, Pen." She passed me the toast rack and marmalade. "Judging by the look on your face, I'd say you finally met Mr. Bancroft."

She knew me so well. "I ran into him yesterday, in fact." I related the gist of the interchange.

She frowned. "Bancroft suspects Eunice of an illicit meeting the night she died?"

"He's too much a gentleman to voice such a notion. I'm extrapolating upon the arc of our conversation."

"Who was she meeting?" Cassie asked.

"My instinct tells me it was Bancroft's secretary—Marsh. Oh, it's not as much of a stretch as you might think," I went on, in response to her skeptical frown. "Joe Marsh is quite the ladies' man and likes to frequent the Forty Steps during his off time. The Collinsworth summer home isn't far from there."

"But a secretary?" Cassie asked incredulously. "It seems unlikely a woman of Eunice Collinsworth's station would carry on so."

"Why—because he's the hired help, or because of her married state? We both know the reverse is common—the married man of the house dallying with a pretty little maid—so why not an older rich woman and a charming, handsome secretary?"

"If true," Cassie said, "Marsh could know something about her death."

"Or even have been the cause of it, whether deliberately or accidentally." I obviously needed to talk with him again, but how was a woman to broach such a delicate subject?

"If the spot is popular with servants on their breaks, wouldn't someone have seen them together? Or at least have seen her fall?"

"Not if it was after the servants had retired...I'm guessing it could have been as late as two or three o'clock in the morning. That's still several hours before Bancroft found her—" I broke off at the sight of Bridget coming in. To my surprise, the dark-haired, wide-shouldered form of Reg Collinsworth was right behind her.

"I invited Reg to breakfast because we're getting an early start today," Bridget explained, no doubt noting our puzzled expressions. "There's much to do."

I was glad I'd eloped. Getting married the conventional way looked to be hard work.

"I thought you were nearly done," Cassie said.

"We have to return to the Newport Club," Collinsworth said.

"Really? But you were just there yesterday," I said.

"The banquet hall ceiling collapsed during the night." He

shrugged. "Must have been all the rain we got the night before last."

"We have to inspect the substitute spaces they're offering," Bridget explained, "and see what will be suitable. Your mother is coming along."

"In light of developments," Collinsworth said, "my sister has renewed her efforts to have us move the wedding to Gull's Bluff." He gave his scowling bride-to-be a sideways glance.

Bridget was spared a reply by the maid coming in with an envelope on a salver.

Collinsworth's face brightened as he grabbed it. "Ah! I've been expecting word from Trent."

"But, sir..." the maid protested. "That's for—"

He'd already slit it open and glanced at the writing before meeting my eye. "Oh. This is for you." He passed it over. "I beg your pardon, Miss Hamilton." His lips twitched in amusement.

He didn't look all that apologetic.

"Excuse me." I left the dining room to read the note in private. Cassie followed me out. I stopped in the corridor and extracted the slip of paper.

Miss Hamilton,

I've made progress in that matter we discussed, but I may have drawn attention to myself in the process. It's best if we're not observed meeting openly. There's an abandoned barn at the edge of the Ashton property. Follow the driveway to the right where it becomes a dirt lane and you'll see it in a mile or so. Ten o'clock tonight.

Yours,

S.

I blew out an exasperated breath. Of all the people to intercept Shaw's note. The detective had been circumspect about the subject at hand, but was it circumspect enough should a guilty man read it?

"Good news, I hope?" Cassie asked, peeking over my shoulder.

I showed it to her before tucking it in my pocket. "It seems promising. Tonight will tell."

With the derringer in my pocket and a lantern in my hand, I followed the dirt road as it wound along the boundary of the Ashton's land. This must have been the original route to the property before the main road had been built to connect with Narragansett Avenue and the center of town. The old lane had not been maintained and was barely passable for vehicles nowadays. Years of successive rains had washed away the under-soil, gouging channels along the edges.

After about twenty minutes of walking I spotted it—a large, dilapidated barn. Visible in the light of a half-moon were a set of splintered wood doors on listing hinges. The roof line dipped along one side, likely having caved in.

When I was a dozen yards away, I stopped and listened. Nothing but the sound of the breeze rustling the branches of the sycamores beyond. I circled the perimeter, stepping carefully among the detritus of branches, stones, and rusted tools. No sign of a horse, bicycle, or conveyance of any kind. Night-blooming jasmine grew in abundance, its scent overpowering in its sweetness. I had to wait for a fit of sneezing to subside before going in. So much for entering by stealth.

I fully opened the lantern shutter and went inside. It looked to be unoccupied, but I searched every stall and behind every trough, just to be sure. It was slow work in the dimness.

I held my lapel watch up to the light. Just on ten o'clock. Shaw might have been delayed, I reasoned, and yet my stomach fluttered with unease. I couldn't shake the sensation that I wasn't alone.

Was that a rustling sound?

I stepped back outside and searched the perimeter again, casting my lantern light as far into the surrounding trees as it could reach, startling an owl from its perch. It flew off in silent reproach.

I was being silly. Of course I wasn't alone. Plenty of night creatures rustle in the brush.

But where was Shaw? I sat upon the remnants of the stone wall beside the lane, rested the derringer in my lap, and waited.

By eleven o'clock I knew he wasn't coming.

I may have drawn attention to myself, he'd said.

I shook off my unease. Any number of reasons could account for his absence.

There was no help for it but to go to bed and hope that tomorrow would bring word from him.

CHAPTER 14

*I*nstead of the dark, sleepy cottage I'd expected upon my return, lights in the front parlor shone in the windows, and as I approached I could see Papa's stout form pacing between them. I hurried to the front door. Was he waiting up for me? I'd told the maid I'd be out and would let myself in. There should have been no cause for alarm.

Of all the possibilities I'd entertained in those moments before I walked into the parlor, seeing my estranged husband, Frank Wynch, standing by the hearth was certainly not one of them.

"Frank! What are you doing here?"

He came toward me. We hadn't spoken in months—since my last case took me to Washington—but the sight of his tall, lanky frame, hazel eyes, and the strong, determined jaw brought back the familiar, conflicting sensations I'd experienced when he'd moved out four years ago.

"Pen." He clasped my hand, his fingers warm through my gloves. He leaned down toward me—he's one of the few men taller than I—and gave me a searching look. "Thank heaven you're all right. Pinkerton and I have been worried about you."

Pinkerton? I blinked and withdrew my hand. "I beg your pardon?"

"You'd better sit down, dear," Papa said, leading me to a seat beside my mother, who moved over with a chilly sniff. "We've been awaiting your return. Where have you been? Cassie said you had an appointment."

"At this ungodly hour," Mother chimed in.

"Never mind that now." I sat. "Just tell me what's going on."

"There's quite a lot to sort out." Papa nodded towards Frank. "Begin again. I'm still trying to make sense of it all."

Frank leaned against the fireplace mantel and propped his foot on the fender. "Monday afternoon, Mr. Pinkerton received an urgent long-distance telephone call from James Gordon Bennett in regards to you."

"Bennett?" I echoed. "How did—? Oh. He must have remembered Lady Ashton's gossip about me. Finally." I glanced over at Mother. "I've been trying to deflect his suspicions for days. I'd counted upon him having been in the throes of an alcoholic haze when he'd first heard it."

"Apparently it was not enough of a haze," Mother shot back, turning her hooked nose and sharp eyes my way. "Your questions about Eunice Collinsworth were too pointed and obviously gave you away."

"There was no mention of a lady by that name," Frank said. "I've been trying to explain, Mrs. Hamilton—Bennett telephoned about another matter entirely." He turned back to me. "Have you been associating with a sneak-thief lately? A blond-haired man, slightly built?"

I recalled Bennett's glare as I parted ways with Shaw outside the sandwich shop. He hadn't known, of course, that Shaw was a private detective rather than a sneak thief. Seeing us together —amicably—must have re-kindled his suspicions about my involvement in the break-in at his estate and had prompted him to act.

"Pen?" Frank prompted.

"Yes I have, but there's an explanation." I looked at my parents. "You two should retire. Frank and I can go over the details in private."

Mother shook her head vigorously. "Absolutely not. I want to know exactly what you've been up to."

"Yes, tell us," Papa urged.

I could see an argument was pointless. I kept my attention upon Frank as I recounted my tale—who Shaw really was, what he'd been up to, how I'd trapped him into revealing himself— his eyebrow lifted in appreciation at that—the check-forging case Shaw was working on, and his agreement to look into the details of Collinsworth's finances.

At mention of the latter, Mother started in her seat. "You asked…a stranger…to look into our private affairs?" she said through gritted teeth.

Even Papa looked perturbed. "There was no need for that, Penelope. I'd already established that Reg Collinsworth is on solid financial footing. I wouldn't have approved the marriage otherwise." He turned briefly to Frank. "My niece is to marry him on Saturday."

"I'm sorry," I said, "but I had to be thorough. We cannot ignore the note."

Frank frowned. "Note?"

I glanced over at Mother. "Show him."

With a heavy sigh, she slipped it out of its hiding place and passed it over.

While Frank was reading it, I continued, "That was sent to the house in Boston before the family left for Newport. As two years have passed since the first wife's death, I haven't been able to make much headway into analyzing the physical circumstances. My best recourse was investigating Collinsworth's possible motive. And greed is a common entice- ment. The first Mrs. Collinsworth was quite wealthy in her own right."

"Did Shaw turn up anything?" Frank asked.

"I've just returned from where we were to meet—an abandoned barn nearby." I made a face. "He never came."

Frank frowned. "That's worrisome."

"In his note this morning, he said his inquiry had attracted attention. He picked an out-of-the-way place tonight for that reason."

"No sign there of anything amiss?" Frank asked.

"Impossible to tell in the dark. I'll check the place more thoroughly tomorrow."

"No." Mother clasped her pale-knuckled hands—the fact that she was gloveless spoke volumes about her degree of agitation. "We must stop this inquiry at once." She turned her piercing gray eyes in my father's direction. "I do not like the idea of our daughter skulking in the dark to meet strange men. It's unseemly."

"And dangerous," Papa added dryly.

I glanced at Frank, whose lips twitched. He was the only other person in the room with a fair idea of the many dark places I'd skulked in.

"Setting aside that issue for the moment," I said, "Frank, tell me—what exactly did Bennett accuse me of? And what did William Pinkerton have to say about it?"

"Pinkerton was circumspect about you, obviously," Frank said. "He neither confirmed nor denied your employment in the face of Bennett's accusations."

"Which were?"

"That you were collaborating with this sneak thief on some unknown scheme. Bennett, of course, knew nothing of Shaw's true identity. None of us did."

"Bennett still doesn't know," I interjected. "Nor does he know about his valet. We must protect Shaw's investigation."

Frank grimaced. "It would be natural for Bennett to assume Shaw's a sneak thief, under the circumstances. You must admit, the man's methods are...well, unorthodox. He broke into two houses and tried to steal the tin from Tompkins in a *bank*, in broad daylight."

"A sneak thief was certainly my original assumption. But it's impossible to explain to Bennett what Shaw is really up to without blowing his case. Bennett himself may be involved, for all we know."

"Yes, it's a possibility," Frank said.

"What was Mr. Pinkerton's response, besides sending you to —what?—keep me in line?"

"No, no, it wasn't that at all," Frank said quickly. "Pinkerton's worried about you. He never considered for a moment that you'd taken up a life of crime."

"Thank heaven for that," I murmured.

"He sent me to find out the real story, and to offer whatever assistance you might require. By all indications, you'd stumbled upon something bigger than you could handle."

I bristled. I wouldn't mind the characterization that I'd *stumbled* upon Shaw's investigation, except for the fact—haven't you noticed?—it's always the *women* doing the stumbling. Heaven forfend the men stumble in the least. No—they *discover* a scheme or *get wise* to a plot. Never stumble.

There was no use fighting semantics. I opted instead to address something else. "This is *not* bigger than I can handle. I managed Shaw just fine. I established what I needed to know about his intent, and enlisted his help in the Collinsworth case."

Mother winced at *Collinsworth case*.

Frank folded his arms, which I know well enough is preparatory to an argument, but I hurried on. "However, I could use your help." I explained what I'd learned so far about the night of Eunice's death, including my recent conversation with Bancroft about his secretary. His narrowed eyes told me I'd piqued his interest.

"You believe the secretary had something to do with Mrs. Collinsworth's death?" he asked.

"Or he at least knows something. I've met Marsh. He's a

smart and personable man. Bancroft himself says he's a great one with the ladies. Perhaps the secretary had a dalliance with Mrs. Collinsworth. But Marsh will not open up to *me* on such a topic. His suspicions would be aroused almost immediately."

Frank brightened. "If I pose as a servant and engage in conversations with Marsh's friends, I'd have a chance to find out more about him. And when Marsh takes his breaks, I can strike up an acquaintance. You say he stays out late?" He checked his watch. "I might even catch him tonight. But I'll need a cover story in place." He eyed my father. "What if you were to hire me—as your driver, perhaps?"

It was an idea worth considering. No one else knew of Frank's relationship to the family—except for Cassie, and she was the soul of discretion—or the fact that he was a private detective.

Papa tapped his chin thoughtfully, but Mother was having none of it. "I do not want *that man* in my house any longer than necessary," she declared.

"Well then, Honoria, you have a choice to make." Papa patted his pockets as he spoke. I suspected he was reflexively groping for his pipe. What man in such a situation wouldn't want to smoke in peace and think over things?

With a sigh, he abandoned the gesture. "Either we attempt to clear the uncertainty hanging over this match between Bridget and Collinsworth, or we send Wynch on his way and drop the matter entirely, never knowing whether our niece has married a murderer."

Mother bit her lip.

"But first"—Papa walked over to Frank—"I have something to say to *you*, sir. You have caused my daughter much grief during your marriage. No, no," he held up a hand to stay Frank's protests, "she hasn't told me anything about it except to say she made a poor match of it, and that the two of you are currently estranged."

At this, Mother gaped in my direction, but I kept my gaze

steadily upon Papa, blinking back the moisture in my eyes. I hadn't wanted this, but here we were. Of all the times for my father to meddle in the affairs of the *female sphere*.

"However," Papa went on, "I know my daughter rather well, and she isn't the only one in the family who can deduce a thing or two. Certain possibilities spring to mind."

Frank looked down at his shoes briefly before meeting my father's stern eye. "It was entirely my doing, sir. I've been trying to make up for it ever since." He turned to look at me. "We aren't such a poor match, Pen. We've worked well together, all in all."

I swallowed. In the early years, it was true. We'd successfully resolved many a case as man and wife back then, sharing the dangers as well as the triumphs. But nothing ever stays the same in life.

When it became obvious I wasn't going to answer, Papa inclined his head in Mother's direction. "What happens next isn't up to you, me, or anyone but Penelope herself." His voice softened as he held my gaze. "What do *you* want, dear?"

I almost laughed aloud. *What do I want?* At the moment, I wanted my lashes to be dry and my nose to stop running. After that, I would be content with an assurance that my cousin wasn't marrying a murderer.

I cleared my throat before trusting my voice. "Hire him, Papa." I stood. "It's been a long evening. I'll say good night now."

CHAPTER 15

Wednesday, June 22nd

I came down late the next morning and inquired closely of the staff as to messages. There was nothing for me—neither from Shaw explaining his absence, nor from Frank as to what progress he may have made in meeting with Marsh last night. With a disappointed sigh, I made my way to the dining room.

I wasn't the only one late to breakfast. My parents had just settled themselves at the table, Papa hiding his yawns behind a newspaper. Mother seemed to have little appetite and only took tea. She tried to catch my eye as I sat at the other end. Probably looking for an opportunity to gloat over my failed marriage.

Well, I wasn't going to give her the chance if I could help it. I had no stomach for breakfast, anyway. I set aside my napkin. "Excuse me."

She followed me out. "Penelope, we need to talk."

I kept walking—out of the house, across the lawn and toward the garden. Away from everyone.

Everyone but my mother, who continued to follow.

I realized the futility of it and stopped at a stone bench at the far end of the lily pond. "All right, Mother. Go ahead. Tell me how foolish I was to elope with Frank. Tell me how I've ruined my life."

She sat upon the bench and patted the space beside her. Reluctantly, I sat.

"That's not what I wanted to say."

I blinked. "It isn't?"

"Of course, I wish you two had not married, but what's done is done. I also wish you'd come and told me you were in trouble. You are too prideful by half."

"Guess who I got that from. What did you want to say, then?"

She turned to face me squarely. "I want to discuss your… problem. We can help you, dear. Papa knows an attorney who can arrange for a quiet divorce. No one in our circle would ever know. You can come back home and start your life over again."

I gaped at her.

"Naturally," she went on, "once we help you find a more suitable prospect for a husband, he would have to know. It's only fair."

"Only fair," I echoed faintly. "Because I'm tainted goods?"

She lifted a shoulder in a half-hearted shrug. "I wouldn't put it as harshly as that."

I rubbed my temples as I felt a headache coming on. "Contrary to what you might believe, I'm content with my life the way it is. I have no wish to 'start over.'"

Her brows tugged together in a skeptical frown. "You cannot mean that. Married to such a man? Reduced to the dangers and indignities of snooping for your livelihood?"

I laughed. "I enjoy the danger, and there's no indignity in helping people." I stood. My headache was lifting, as it often does when long-sought clarity comes. "As to my marriage, that's between me and my husband."

Mother was shaking her head. "I will never understand you, Penelope."

"I know."

I left her to stare meditatively at the pond. I had a barn to search.

I ran into Cassie on my way back in to fetch my hat.

"Pen! How was your meeting with Shaw?" she asked. "Your mother woke me last night, asking where you were. Is everything all right?"

"Shaw never came. He hasn't sent word, either."

"There could be an innocuous explanation."

"I'm going back to look around. Want to come with me for a bit of detecting?"

"That's the most interesting prospect I've had all week. Give me a minute to change into sturdier shoes."

Soon we were heading down the dirt lane toward the old barn. I'd wanted Cassie with me not only because of her sharp eyes, but also to catch her up on Frank's arrival. She has been my steadfast friend through all of my marital difficulties. Not surprisingly, she holds my estranged husband in little regard.

She stopped short in the road when I broke the news. "You can't be serious."

"It's true. Gordon Bennett contacted Mr. Pinkerton, who sent Frank." I explained that Bennett had for days been on the brink of remembering Lady Ashton's gossip about me being a detective. "Unfortunately, I supplied one of the missing pieces, when I mentioned I was from Chicago. Bennett finally put the two together and knew which office to call."

"Still, it seems rather extreme to place a long-distance telephone call to Chicago just to complain about you," she objected.

"Not so extreme for a rich and well-connected newspaper magnate," I said, as we resumed walking. "He has many such resources at his fingertips. He assumed the worst when he saw me and Shaw together and wanted to get to the bottom of the matter." I smiled to myself. William Pinkerton, of course, hadn't given him quite what he'd wanted.

"So Pinkerton sent Frank to check on you? Now what? I hope he's not staying."

"He's helping us with the inquiry into Eunice's death. He'll be posing as our driver. That way he can mingle with the other servants at the Forty Steps during their breaks and try to learn something."

"Ah." Her forehead cleared in understanding. "About Marsh in particular?"

"Exactly."

"Well, it's an ill wind that blows no good—" She stopped again as we reached the curve in the lane and she got her first look at the dilapidated structure. "*This* is where you were to meet Shaw?" She shivered, looking over the caved roof, broken doors, and tangle of vines among the debris. "I shouldn't like to be alone here in the dark. It's too far away for anyone to hear you scream and come to your rescue."

"Fortunately, I had no need to scream," I said dryly. "Come on, let's look around."

"What are we looking for?"

"Any indication that someone besides myself has been here recently. Trash, horse droppings, wheel marks, footprints—that sort of thing. I'm wondering if Shaw came ahead of our appointed time but was followed. He might have realized it and decided to abandon our meeting." If so, who had followed him? Collinsworth? He'd seen the note.

"All right, then." Cassie picked up a long stick and began poking among the thick brush between the rock wall and the edge of the lane. I left her to it and went inside the building.

Mourning doves preened along the rafters near the open end of the roof. The mid-morning sun streamed through that section, forming long, dust-mote-riddled bands across the space. Now that the night flowers had closed their petals, other scents were becoming evident—rust, axle grease, and animal droppings.

I didn't find anything of interest until I searched the center stall. Here the dust had been disturbed with blurred footprints. I sifted aside clumps of hay and found a man's brown shoe, scuffed and worn at the heel. Nearby, I caught a glint of something gold in the light.

I'd just crouched down for a better look when the sound of Cassie's scream sent me running outside.

She stood at the far side of the lane, white faced and trembling.

I put my arms around her thin shoulders and guided her over to the low rock wall to sit down. "Take deep breaths. Yes, that's right…. Better?"

Her shivering subsided.

"Where?" I asked. Only one thing could have frightened her so.

She pointed toward a swale behind a stand of trees, where a pile of leaves had drifted.

Mouth dry, I went over for a look. At first, I wasn't sure what initially drew her attention, until I saw the shoeless foot. I knelt at the other end of the pile, gingerly brushing leaves aside until I'd uncovered the back of the head—blond—and the shoulders of the man. A fish-gutting knife stuck out of his back, just beneath his ribs. His taupe gabardine jacket was saturated with blood.

Reason told me it could only be Shaw, but I had to know for sure. I cleared more leaf debris from his torso and turned him on his side to see his face.

Yes, it was he. I sat back on my heels and blew out a long, slow breath.

"Pen?" Cassie's tentative voice called. She was heading toward me. I got up, quickly brushed off my skirt, and intercepted her before she got too close.

"I'm sorry I screamed. I'm all right now." She gestured toward the body. "Is it…Shaw?"

"I'm afraid so. Murdered sometime before I arrived last night, most likely. I waited quite a while and he never came."

"What do we do now?"

"Are you feeling well enough to return to the cottage on your own? Good. Have Papa send for the police, and ask Frank to join me here in the meantime."

"You're staying? Alone?"

"Whoever's responsible has long gone. Besides, I don't want to leave him." The scavenger animals wouldn't be far behind. Shaw deserved better.

She bit her lip. "I'll be as quick as I can."

I watched her hurry away, leaving me in the deep shadows of the thicket. Despite my reassurances, I wished I'd brought my gun.

CHAPTER 16

$\mathcal{I}$ never thought I'd feel such relief at the sight of Frank's wiry form and his rapid, long-legged strides as he hastened along the lane. Stepping into his strong arms for comfort felt so natural. After a moment, I remembered myself and pulled back.

"This was my fault," I said, wiping my eyes on my sleeve. "He wouldn't have been here except for me."

Frank shook his head. "He knew the risks." He stepped around me for a better look at the body. "Besides, we don't know if he was killed for what he'd discovered about Collinsworth, or because of the case he was originally working on."

"I don't know, Frank. Someone dealing in bad checks is an entirely different criminal than the murderer of a defenseless woman like Eunice Collinsworth."

He frowned. "*Any* man who feels deeply threatened is dangerous, whether or not he starts out as a murderer. Shaw obviously got too close for comfort one way or another. We don't want to narrow the possibilities too soon."

I could see his point.

He crouched beside the body, shifted aside the rest of the leaves, then searched through the pockets.

"Anything?" I asked.

"Every pocket's empty. Our killer was thorough." He scratched his head beneath his cap as he looked over the corpse. "Have you seen the other shoe?"

"In the barn. I thought I saw something else, but was interrupted when Cassie screamed."

He stood and brushed off his knees. "Let's go look."

I led him to the stall, pointing to the shoe. "It matches the other one."

Frank picked it up with a grunt.

I stepped around the marks on the floor. "You see the scuffs in the dust? It looks like the struggle happened here. The killer was waiting to ambush Shaw."

"That seems likely," Frank said. "You said you saw something else here in the stall?"

"A bit of metal." I crouched amid the clump of hay that had drifted to the side, feeling around. "Ah, found it." I brought it over to the light.

"A gold cufflink," Frank said.

My heart sank. "With an onyx stone inlay. Reg Collinsworth has a set similar to this, though I didn't get a good look at the time."

"It's not an uncommon style," Frank pointed out. "But Collinsworth didn't know about your meeting with Shaw, did he?"

"Actually, he intercepted Shaw's note at breakfast yesterday before realizing it was for me. I wasn't particularly worried at the time—Shaw was cryptic in his wording and only signed his name with an initial."

"Still, it's a worrisome coincidence," Frank admitted. "Particularly if the cufflink turns out to be Collinsworth's."

A rapid clattering brought us outside. A black coach was coming toward us at as quick a pace as the condition of the road would allow.

"How much do we tell them?" Frank murmured in my ear.

I bit my lip. Good question. "We should at least provide the poor man's name. And give them the cufflink. But sharing our conjectures would unleash more questions than we're prepared to answer right now."

Frank nodded. "With the cufflink in hand, the police can check for its mate."

"Among all the jewel boxes of all the local males of Newport society?" I said skeptically. One gentleman's personal effects, however, I was determined to search for myself. Getting into Reg Collinsworth's bedroom undetected would require careful planning.

Three policemen climbed out of the coach and advanced toward us.

"How do we tell them it's Shaw without revealing the rest of it?" I murmured. "I'm drawing a blank."

Frank gave a quick wink. "I have an idea."

Officer Jance of the Newport Police was a burly fellow of advancing age, judging by the flecks of gray in his shaggy muttonchops and the deep creases in the corners of his eyes. His glance settled on me briefly when we exchanged perfunctory introductions. He turned to Frank. "Where?"

"This way."

I made to follow when Jance put up a hand. "No need to trouble you, miss. You may return to your home. No sense becoming further involved in such a sordid business. I'll have some questions for you later, naturally, but the gentleman here can supply me with most of what I need."

I scowled.

"I didn't find the body," Frank pointed out. "Miss— Hamilton and her friend did."

"I cannot abide female hysterics," Jance snapped. "It's best if the young lady waits at home."

Hysterics, indeed.

But I was more than ready for a comfortable chair and a hot cup of tea, to be honest. And something to eat—I'd never had breakfast and missed lunch. I smiled sweetly at the policeman. "I'll be at Ashton cottage when you require me, Officer."

I returned to find Cassie anxiously pacing the brick-lined drive in front of the cottage. Her face brightened. "Pen! Thank heaven. Where's Frank?"

"He and the police will be along in a bit." I dropped my voice. "Do you think Mrs. Mullins would mind if I raided her larder?"

Cassie linked her arm through mine. "Not at all. Let's go."

Mrs. Mullins, bless her, fussed over us as she would lost children—fetching extra chairs from the housekeeper's sitting room, setting the kettle to boil, pulling out cheese and chutney and thick slices of fresh bread.

"Poor lambs," she said, shaking her head toward us as she slid over the cheese plate. "How dreadful to find a dead man! Lord knows what this world is coming to." She looked at us with a gleam in her green eyes. "Did ya know him? Wot was he doing there?"

I waved a hand in a helpless gesture. "All I can tell you, Mrs. Mullins, is we were out for a stroll near the old barn this morning and simply...stumbled upon him."

Now, *that's* when "stumbling" should be used.

Cassie flashed me a look and coughed into her napkin.

"The barn...that old eyesore!" Mrs. Mullins clucked her tongue. "Lord Ashton's been taking his sweet time getting it torn down. Though you didn' hear that from me," she added with a sly wink.

"How long has it been abandoned?" I asked.

She leaned forward and added another generous dollop of rhubarb chutney to my plate. I flashed her a grateful look. It was good chutney.

"Eight years, maybe? When they put in the new road that

connected all the estates along this stretch. Lord Ashton built a new barn and carriage house closer to the road."

So the old barn was an out-of-the-way place known only to locals. Shaw, of course, as a thorough investigator would have explored the Ashton grounds when he first had me under suspicion.

Finally, I pushed back my plate. "That was delicious, Mrs. Mullins. Thank you."

The sound of raised voices reached our ears through the open kitchen window to the patio beyond.

"*Of course* I want to marry you!" It was Bridget. "But something is very wrong. I can feel it. You've been acting oddly for the past week, Reg. And you have to admit, we've been arguing more than we ever have."

Mrs. Mullins quietly carried the cutting board over to the sink beneath the window. She took quite a while there, brushing off invisible crumbs.

"I admit no such thing." Collinsworth's voice had an edge to it. "We've more problems to deal with lately, that's all—the damage to my surrey, the break-in, and now there's the unusable banquet hall, and—"

"And," Bridget cut in, "a man has been killed. How can we possibly carry on as if nothing is—" Her voice broke off in a sob.

"Bridget, dear, none of that matters." His voice was pleading. "We didn't know the poor fellow. This has nothing to do with us."

"We should postpone the wedding." Bridget's voice was strained. "For a little while, at least."

"Now, now," came Papa's jovial voice. "What's this I hear about postponing?"

The voices got quieter after that. Mrs. Mullins finally left her post and came back over to us. "Miss Bridget is mighty upset. She just walked off. Poor lamb"— she broke off as Frank strode into the kitchen.

He gave a deferential bow, his expression servile. "Miss Hamilton, Miss Leigh, there's a policeman wanting to see you. He's in the drawing room."

"Yes, of course," I said.

Frank led the way down the corridor.

I hurried up behind him. "What did you tell Jance?" I whispered.

"That I knew Shaw professionally," he murmured back. "It seemed to do the trick."

"What?" I reflexively grabbed his sleeve. "You told him you're a Pinkerton?"

"It was the only way to convince him. But I professed ignorance as to what Shaw was working on."

"Did Jance ask about your case?"

"Yes, but he didn't press after I told him I wasn't at liberty to say. I assured him it wasn't related to Shaw."

I dearly hoped that was true. I dropped my hand. "He doesn't know we're married, does he?"

A look of irritation crossed his face briefly. "No."

"What about the cufflink?" I asked.

"He took possession of it, naturally. I'm not sure whether he considers it important or not. He wasn't exactly forthcoming with me."

Cassie, bless her, had gone on ahead to afford us privacy. But she stopped suddenly.

Mother was standing in front of the drawing room door. She looked past Cassie, glaring at Frank.

"Hmm, well—I have work to do," Frank said. "See you later, Pen." He made a quick exit, skirting past my scowling mother.

"Penelope," she said, "may I have a private word?"

I hesitated. "Cassie, you go on in. Tell Officer Jance I'll be there shortly."

Mother pulled me farther from the door after Cassie shut it behind her. "What are you going to tell that policeman?" she hissed.

"I would like to tell him everything," I retorted, "but you're obviously here to forbid that."

"The police cannot know about you investigating Bridget's fiancé, or that you asked that-that detective—Shaw—to help you. Remember, you work for *me*. I'm entitled to confidentiality, am I not?"

"I'll do my best, but it may be unavoidable. Shaw had learned something. He was killed before he could tell me. My withholding the information about why he was at the barn last night could allow his killer to go free."

Her eyes narrowed. "Shaw could have met his unfortunate end for any number of reasons."

"I know that—and this reason is among them."

"Please?" She smoothed her skirt with trembling hands. "These events have agitated everyone. Your father has Collinsworth in his study, trying to settle him down, Bridget went off in a huff to heaven knows where…I don't want to make things worse."

I blew out a breath. "All right. I'll keep it to myself. *For now.* That's all I can promise." Thank goodness Frank had already smoothed the way in that regard. But at what cost? I was uneasy about that.

The parlor door opened, and Officer Jance stuck out his grizzled head. "Ah, Miss Hamilton! If you would join us, please." He stepped out, holding the door expectantly.

I gave her one last look over my shoulder as I went in.

I had only to affect sufficient feminine ignorance and distress for Jance to confine his questioning to the minimal details of our discovery of Shaw. With Cassie taking my cue—accompanied by the judicious application of a handkerchief to her eye—he'd soon released us.

"Well, that wasn't so bad," Cassie said, re-pinning her hat as we stepped outside. "I'm going to take a turn in the rose garden to clear my head. Want to join me?"

"No thanks. I'm going to check on Bridget."

Finally, after ascertaining my cousin had gone up to change and left with her geological tools, I located her along the shingle of rock formations known to locals as Conrad's Cave. As I passed the Forty Steps, empty of servants at this time in the afternoon but still busy with sea-bathers heading to and from the shore, I realized I'd forgotten to ask Frank if he'd had a chance to speak with Marsh last night. The problem of Shaw's murder had occupied me completely.

Conrad's Cave isn't much of a cave these days—more of a depression in the cliff face. As it was only accessible at low tide, the interior was still quite soggy. I took off my shoes and stockings first before going in.

Bridget was on her hands and knees, heedless of the puddles, plying a small chisel to carefully release something from a rocky outcropping. The sound of the waves masked my approach, so I called out a greeting in order not to startle what was obviously delicate work.

She sat back on her heels, flashing me a brief look of annoyance.

"Need any help?" I asked, crouching next to her.

"You can hold the bag," she answered curtly, passing over a small canvas pouch.

I watched as she pried a chunk of rock from the cliff face. "What is that? It looks as if something's imprinted upon it."

"It's a fossil in the sedimentary rock. An arthropod of some sort." She tilted it toward the light for me to see the impression of a small, insect-like creature. "It's not complete, but you can see some of the limbs and the carapace." She dropped it in and dusted off her gloves. "Did Reg send you to talk sense into me?"

"I haven't seen him. Besides, you're far more sensible than he."

"He *can* behave like a little boy at times," she mused, "preoccupied with his expensive toys and amusements, petulant when things don't go his way."

There seemed no good answer to that, so I let her talk.

"And then there's his reckless side," she went on. "I hate it when he shows off for the sake of his friends."

I knew my next question was an impertinent one, but I asked it anyway, since that's what cousins do. "Why marry him, then?"

She gave a bitter laugh as she stood and collected her tools. "I've asked myself the same question." She met my eye, and her expression softened. "My answer is the same as that of any other woman who marries a flawed man, in spite of reasons not to. I love him."

I hoped her fiancé's flaws didn't include murdering his first wife and now a detective.

At my lengthy silence, she touched my arm and said earnestly, "Believe it or not, Reg has many good things to recommend him. You don't know him as I do. He can be funny, brave, and generous. And he puts up with *my* eccentricities. I'm by no means perfect." She gestured to her bag. "What man would give his bride-to-be excavating tools as an engagement present? Not many, I suspect."

There was no denying that. "Are you going to postpone the wedding?" I asked.

She brushed away a dark strand of hair with her work glove, leaving a dirt smear across her forehead. "You heard?"

"It was hard not to. You two have been arguing a great deal lately, in fact."

"Wedding jitters, I suppose. I was too heated at the time to continue the discussion. Now that I'm calmer I can see it's best to continue with the ceremony as planned. I *am* sorry about the dead man. But as Reg says, it has nothing to do with us."

"What if it's more than jitters, Bridget? You shouldn't marry him out of a misguided sense of obligation."

"That's not it." Her eyes took on a faraway look. "The inescapable fact of it is, Pen, he's a part of me now. I could no less painfully separate myself from my arm as I could walk out of his life."

133

Profound words from one so young. I sighed and looked out toward the bay. *I could no less painfully separate myself....*

In that moment, I realized why the estrangement between Frank and I could not be solved by a quiet divorce. We might never again live together as man and wife, but Frank was indeed an inextricable part of me, of my life. And I very much wanted that life, as tumultuous and hazardous and unsettling as it could be. I could never go back to the constraint and tedium of Mother's world.

"Pen?" Bridget worried voice broke into my thoughts. "Are you all right?" She gently touched my cheek. "Your face is wet."

"Must be the salt spray." I sniffed and fished for a handkerchief. "Shall we go back?"

"Just a moment. I'm nearly done."

I looked around idly as she finished cleaning off her tools and packing them away. The space was obviously used by young boys, evidenced by a broken-handled slingshot in the corner, stacks of flat rocks forming a rough platform against the cliff wall, and discarded tin cans scattered about. Some were rusted, some were newer...all were scratched up, no doubt from the pummeling of sling-shot pebbles.

One tin—and a bit of a blue label—caught my eye.

Bridget looked over as I picked it up. "All sorts of debris in here."

"The local boys likely raid the nearby rubbish bins for cans to use as target practice," I mused aloud, trying to keep my voice even while my heart pounded with excitement at the sight of the words *Mrs. Acker's Custom Blended Coffee*. The label was stained and partly ripped from rough handling. I could see another layer of paper beneath.

I'd better wait to examine it in private.

"You're taking that bit of trash with you?" Bridget asked incredulously.

I smiled. "Cassie needs more pots for her cuttings."

CHAPTER 17

Officer Jance had gone by the time we returned. Collinsworth, thankfully, had also gone, which spared Bridget an awkward encounter. She headed upstairs to change for afternoon tea while I went looking for Frank.

Since he was continuing the pretense of being in the Hamiltons' employ, I first tried the carriage house. One lad coiling a hose tipped his cap as I passed. I found Frank crouched upon the garage floor, plying an oil can to the springs of a brougham.

"Pen!" His eyes lit up as he got to his feet. "You haven't been talking to Jance all this time, have you?"

"No, he's gone. I spent some time with Bridget. Naturally she's distressed by the discovery of a body on the grounds."

He made a face as he wiped his hands on a grease rag. "Without a doubt. How was your interview with Jance?"

"Mother has tied my hands," I fumed. "She's forbidden me to tell the police about the accusation against Collinsworth, and of Shaw's involvement. I had to stick with your story and resort to wide-eyed innocence."

He chuckled in sympathy.

"But I've made progress in another area, at least." I held up the coffee can. "I found this near the Cliff Walk. It's what Shaw was looking for."

Intrigued, he followed me out of the building to a sunlit bench. I slipped my finger under the wrapper, gently tugging. I felt more paper beneath and carefully extricated two intact slips. They were, indeed, bank checks. The first belonged to a Mrs. Winslow Daniels and the second to a Mr. Joseph Matthews. Each was about a year old, properly endorsed by the account holder, and bore a cancelation stamp.

Joseph Matthews. I pursed my lips. Matthews…Matthews… where had I heard the name?

"Well?" Frank's voice broke into my thoughts. He was impatiently breathing over my shoulder for a better look.

"Oh! Sorry." I passed them over.

"Ah, the canceled checks. This is what Shaw attempted to steal from Tompkins when you stopped him at the bank?"

"That's right. Tompkins was to copy them. I imagine he would have returned them the same way, so they could be restored to their owners on the sly."

"You don't know who gave Tompkins the coffee tin?"

"Shaw wouldn't tell me." But now I remembered where I'd heard Matthews's name.

"What do we do now?" he asked.

What *were* we going to do? I had an idea.

"Pen?" he prompted, as I stood and stuffed the checks in my pocket.

"I'll tell you on the way. Let me fetch my lockpicks."

"Lockpicks?" he echoed. "Where are we going?"

"Shaw's room at Ocean House." I prayed he'd left his logbook there last night, rather than carrying it upon his person for the murderer to take. And that the police hadn't found his lodgings yet.

On the drive there, it didn't take long to recount my idea. One wastes few words explaining things to a quick-witted man such as Frank.

"What's your plan for getting in to search his room?" he asked, as we turned onto Bellevue.

"I thought the direct approach would work best. Do you still have the pocket knife I gave you?"

He grunted, shifted the reins to one hand, and pulled it out of his jacket pocket.

"Thanks." I turned it over. The silver had tarnished over the years, but the mahogany wood inlay had aged well. It had been my first anniversary gift to him. Thank heaven I'd never gotten around to having it monogrammed, or the plan wouldn't work at all.

"You're going to use the he-dropped-this ploy to find out his room number?" he asked.

"Maybe."

"*Hmph.* I'd like to get that back, you know." His voice was gruff with sentiment.

"I'll have to see what approach I want to use. But if I have to sacrifice it, I'll get you a new one," I promised.

He grumbled under his breath as we pulled up to the Ocean House hotel.

"Park farther down the street after you let me out. I'll catch up with you there."

His hazel eyes narrowed with worry. "Any sign of trouble, Pen, don't wait. Get out of there."

I nodded, my throat inexplicably constricting at the concern in his voice.

I climbed down, smoothed my dress, and walked into the lobby.

The seaside décor was impossible to miss, from the large wall mural of a shoreline scene to the brightly striped cushioned chairs to even a series of stuffed seagulls atop occasional tables. I suppressed a grimace.

A short, rotund woman with a faded floral apron and a matronly air looked up at my approach. "Hello, Miss. Do you have a reservation?"

The proprietress's sharp-eyed demeanor made me abandon the he-dropped-this ploy. I gave her a smile. "I'm not looking for a room, but for a gentleman who's staying here. Johnny Sharpe? He's a cousin of mine."

Did I mention that cousins were plentiful this season?

"Cousin?" She narrowed her eyes. "We run a decent establishment here. I can't be sending up every strange woman who claims to be a man's *cousin.*" She shook her head, muttering, "Or strange man, neither."

Strange man…had Collinsworth come ahead of me, with the same purpose in mind? "Excuse me," I interjected, "you say a man came to see him today? Tall, dark-haired, with a cleft in his chin?"

The woman's frown deepened. "No—this fella was shorter'n me. Wavy reddish-brown hair. *He* said he was a cousin, too."

So, not Reg Collinsworth. I dearly wanted to ask for more details, but I'd already aroused her suspicions. I gave a casual shrug. "Well, I have no idea who that could be. I'm the only cousin Johnny has in this world."

She looked me up and down. "Sorry, miss, but I don't see a family resemblance. Mr. Sharpe's slim like you, but a good bit shorter, I recollect. "

"He never liked to drink his milk as a child, much to the vexation of his poor mother." I removed my hat and patted my light blond hair. "We do possess the distinctive Sharpe family hair, however."

She grinned. "That you do!" She smoothed her gray hair self-consciously. "I was fair-haired myself, back in the day. Always wanted a little girl with bright blond curls…ah, well."

I put my hat back on. "Can I go up and see him?"

Her teeth tugged at her lower lip as she considered. "I'm not sure he's in. That one keeps all kinds of odd hours. I meant to go check on him after that other fella left, but I've been so busy down here. Lemme go up first—oh, hang on a minute—as soon as I'm finished here." She turned as another patron approached, bags in tow. "Yes, sir?" She swiped a stray lock from her damp forehead. "Of course, sir, let me get the book"—

"You're busy enough as it is, ma'am," I broke in. "Let me save you the trouble. What room is it?"

"Hmm?" she looked up from turning the pages of the register for the new guest to sign. "Oh…Room 22. Thank you, dear."

Shaw's room was next to the side stairwell on the second floor. The timing was fortunate, as most of the patrons were either on the veranda enjoying afternoon refreshments or still out sea-bathing. I opened my lockpicks case and set to work, only once having to duck into the stairwell when I heard footsteps.

I experienced that familiar thrill of anticipation when I heard a faint *click* and the knob turned in my hand.

I quickly slipped inside.

The door nearly hit the end of the bed in the tiny room. Hardly a surprise, as the establishment was rather pricey for Shaw's budget. He would have picked the least-expensive room for rent. I closed the door and flipped the inner latch.

The long curtains were drawn across the French doors to the balcony beyond. I pulled one aside, just enough to peek out. This room faced the street—no view to speak of, unless one enjoyed watching the evening promenade of the affluent. I could see Frank's buggy, parked farther down the street in front of an empty band stand.

I turned back to the room. The plain iron bed was neatly made. The only other furniture in the room was a rocking chair, a washstand with pitcher and basin, and a small chest of draw-ers. That seemed the best place to start.

It took me a while to find Shaw's logbook—he'd been as circumspect as I am about concealing mine—but I finally located it in the false bottom of his battered suitcase.

My heart beat faster as I turned over the brown leather

volume in my hands. This was indeed the book he'd been writing in the day I'd confronted him.

My original plan was to find the book, take it away with me, and peruse it safely back at the cottage. But all I really needed from it was what Shaw had discovered about Collinsworth. It seemed heartless to take the entire record of the man's work, especially when he was so close to solving the check-forging case. The agency he worked for would want it now.

Staying longer was a risk, but I sat on the bed and flipped to the last few entries, scanning for what he'd learned from his investment broker friend about Collinsworth.

Here was something.

June 20th

Talked with M today on new client's behalf. He was guarded at first—the wealthy don't like to tell tales about others in their set —but I'd done him a big favor last year and he knew it.

It turns out C had gotten into a spot of trouble in the summer of '85 when a string of large gambling debts finally caught up to him. C came to M for a sizeable loan, which he'd given him. But two weeks later an angry and mortified Mrs. C came to M with full repayment of the loan. M later learned she'd sold her brownstone in New York to manage it.

Throughout that summer, speculation circulated whenever the couple was observed behaving in chilly fashion towards one another at parties, though no one but M knew why. Not sure this will be helpful to new client, as the matter was resolved before Mrs. C's death. But I'll pass along the information tonight, as promised.

M was actually more helpful to me in my own case. I was forthcoming with him as to what I was working on. Previous experience has shown I can count upon his discretion. I did, however, withhold the name of B's valet so as not to place M in an awkward position. (I had to withhold another name for the same reason when speaking to new client).

As I explained my case, M grew alarmed and pulled out a strong box from his desk drawer. That morning he'd noticed a canceled check was missing.

I took a breath. A missing check and an investment broker with the initial M. Matthews, the signatory on the second check I'd found? I turned the page.

After close inquiry I was able to narrow the opportunity for the theft to a house party the family had given on June 15th. M gave me a copy of the guest list, which is in the back of this logbook. R was on it, and I'm now absolutely certain that he is running the check-forging operation. M is a sharp-witted fellow and saw me lingering over the name. I refused to confirm it when he asked me point-blank.

I looked up from my reading. Many names begin with *R*…but this was a name Shaw had withheld from me, to avoid "an awkward position." Awkward how? Probably because I knew the person.

Shaw had said it was a man with servants. If one were to assume it was a risk-taking, reckless man, a man who craved wealth—and perhaps envied the good life of his friend, Reginald Collinsworth?—then I only knew of one fellow.

Reeves. A shortish man with wavy, reddish-brown hair. So, he'd been after Shaw's logbook, too.

I bit back a sigh and resumed reading.

T was not in attendance at M's that night, though he had been at parties hosted by two previous victims.

I pursed my lips. T—for Trent, of course. He'd mentioned the Matthews party as among the tiresome affairs he'd had the good fortune to miss.

The reason may have to do with the argument I'd overheard between them last week, detailed in an earlier entry, where I also describe what I learned about R and T living beyond their means as a motive for the scheme.

I resisted the urge to flip back to that section. I needed to finish this part, leave the book, and get out. The matron at the front desk would come up any minute to check on me here. I browsed through the rest more quickly.

M of course knows what precautions to take against spurious bank drafts, so I'm not concerned for his pocketbook. After extracting his promise to keep his speculations about the culprit confidential, I headed back to town, but then realized I was being followed. The man in question drove a closed-top buggy and kept his hat brim low. I couldn't identify him. I managed to evade him and return to the hotel.

Once I speak with new client about this side matter, I'll complete my report and turn over my evidence on the check-forging ring to the agency. I wish I'd found the coffee tin, but new client may have better luck. I'll provide the address to contact if it turns up later.

If the man following Shaw from Matthews' cottage had been Reeves—or someone hired by him—what would Reeves have done next? He hadn't been able to lay his hands on the canceled checks that Tompkins had lost. That must have been profoundly worrisome....

A memory stirred. I'd run into Reeves coming out of the kitchen at the Ashton cottage, just before our outing along the promenade. Had he been looking for the tin then? His colleague, Tompkins, had no doubt told him of the initial attempt by Shaw to steal it at the bank, and then Bennett gifting the coffee to me.

With Shaw's visit to Matthews, Reeves might have assumed the detective finally had the canceled checks in his possession and was making inquiries to narrow down the possibilities. He would have to be stopped.

Thank goodness I hadn't embroiled Reg Collinsworth in Shaw's death, after all. I didn't know how to account for the cuff-link yet—or even if it was his—but in light of Shaw's discoveries it had to be Reeves who'd killed Shaw. Of course, that meant Reeves would have needed to know Shaw was going to meet me at the barn last night, but I had a good idea how he'd found out.

I jumped at the knock on the door.

"Mr. Sharpe, are you in there?" the matron's voice called.

"Foolish woman!" a man's voice said impatiently, "I told you —he's *dead*. Now unlock this door, if you please. I must search the premises."

I froze. Officer Jance. He'd found the lodging more quickly than I'd expected.

"I'm sorry, sir," the woman said, her voice meek. "Force of habit, I suppose."

I left Shaw's logbook—thank heaven he'd acceded to my request to keep all references to me out of it—pulled the canceled checks out of my pocket and laid them on top, then skittered over to the balcony doors.

"Lemme find the right key," the matron said. "Poor, poor man."

I heard the key jingle in the lock, but the inner bolt held fast.

There was a muffled exclamation but I didn't stay to hear more. I hurried out to the balcony and straddled the railing.

I shifted my attention away from the wide-eyed stares of the people on the sidewalk and surveyed the terrain below. The bushes looked full enough to soften my landing.

I jumped, detangled myself less than gracefully from the shrubbery, and strode briskly towards Frank's waiting coach.

He saw me coming and opened the door.

"Let's go," I panted.

He tapped the reins. "You have leaves in your hair."

"You saw?"

"As did many people. Where's your hat?"

Drat. "Back in the bushes, I expect. At least I have your pocket knife." I passed it over.

"Did you find the logbook?"

"Yes. I was just finishing with it when the police arrived."

He shot me a look. "You left it there?"

"Along with the canceled checks. It seemed the best course of action. Jance can take it from there."

"It was Jance who came? Did he see you?"

"I don't think so, but it won't take him long to figure it out." I'd worry about accounting for myself when I had to. In the meantime, I had another idea. "Do you know where Trent's house is?"

He nodded. "We're going there next, I take it?"

CHAPTER 18

$\mathcal{I}$'d picked the remaining vegetation off my person and had recounted to Frank what I'd read in Shaw's logbook by the time we passed through Trent's front gate. The estates along this stretch weren't as large as those along Bellevue, but judging from the stone lions flanking the columned porch and the crenelated parapet on the third story, it wasn't cheap to maintain.

"Shouldn't I come in with you?" Frank asked, helping me down. "He may try to flee once he knows the jig is up."

"I have questions about Collinsworth that only he can answer. He'll be more forthcoming if I talk with him alone. But I appreciate you keeping an eye out while I'm inside." I put a hand on Frank's arm, which he reflexively tightened. "It turns out I do need your help, after all."

His gaze was long and appreciative, but all he said was, "William Pinkerton is a wise man."

The maid, with a puzzled glance at my hatless appearance —or perhaps a few leaves had escaped my notice—escorted me to the parlor while she went to fetch her master.

Trent came in a few minutes later. He bowed politely, pushing back the ever-present shock of straight brown hair from his eyes. "Miss Hamilton, how kind of you to come by! I'm afraid I can only spare a minute. I'm about to call upon Rebecca—Miss Blakeley, I mean—and take her for a drive."

"I won't be long, but it's urgent that we talk."

"Of course." He waved me into a chair and took one himself.

"It seems your friends—Collinsworth and Reeves—have been taxing your conscience a great deal lately," I began.

He blinked. "I beg your pardon?"

"I have reason to believe the police will soon take Donald Reeves into custody for running a check-forging operation."

He shifted uneasily in his chair. "Reeves? How is that possible?"

"You heard about the man who died yesterday—Shaw?"

"Yes. Poor fellow."

"He was a private detective who'd been investigating the check-forging scheme," I said. "A written account of his discoveries in the case, along with the most recent canceled checks given to Tompkins to copy, are now in the hands of the police."

"B—but—what have I to do with that?" Trent stammered.

I glared. "Do not insult my intelligence, sir."

He looked down at his hands.

I waited.

Finally, he met my eye. "I'm not proud of it. About ten days ago I told Reeves he was on his own. I wanted no part of it anymore. You may not believe me, but it's true."

"My believing you is immaterial. It is the authorities you must convince."

He flinched. "How do you come to know of it?"

"That, too, is immaterial," I said tartly. "Of more import is why you involved yourself in such a sordid scheme."

"I keep asking myself that very question. Reeves has a way of talking a fellow into things. It didn't seem so terrible, at first. These are extremely wealthy people who wouldn't feel the loss at all. My role was minimal. I was to simply distract any guests who might be headed toward the host's study while Don was in there."

I felt a chill as a terrible thought occurred to me. "Did Reeves talk Reg Collinsworth into the scheme, too?"

"Why? He doesn't need the money as we do." His frown cleared. "Ah. You must have heard about Reg's gambling debts. Those were settled long ago."

"By his first wife?"

His ears reddened and he cleared his throat. "In a manner of speaking. Once she died…at least, that's what I—I assume."

So he didn't know about Matthews' loan and Eunice selling her townhouse to pay it off. I eyed Trent, who shifted uncomfortably in the silence.

If Trent had lied for Collinsworth the night his wife died, as I suspected he had, what then? Had Trent later worried his friend had killed his wife? What would he have done once Collinsworth prepared to marry again?

I had a hunch. "Did you write the anonymous note my mother received?"

He abruptly got up from his chair, pacing between the bookcase and the window.

It was answer enough. "When the police found Collinsworth with you and broke the news of Eunice's death," I said, "you corroborated his account that he'd been there with you all night long. But that wasn't true, was it?"

Trent shoved his hands in his pockets. "He didn't arrive until early morning."

"You're referring to your Portsmouth residence, correct?" From Newport, that was a drive of only a few hours. "Did he tell you where he'd been?"

"There's a gaming den in Portsmouth he liked to frequent. He said he'd argued with his wife, left in a huff, and ended up there. When he couldn't break his losing streak he gave up and came to see me."

"Once the police came, he asked you to lie for him?"

"He didn't have to ask. I merely took his cue. We both knew how bad it would look for him to have been out gambling while his wife had fallen to her death. Especially after he'd already racked up considerable debt and had promised he was done with it."

"But later you came to doubt his story. Why?"

He ran a hand across the back of his neck in a weary gesture. "After her will was settled, Reg acted more guilty than grieved. I began to wonder. After all, he'd told me himself that they'd argued that day. And he avoided me for months after her death."

"Your friend had plenty to feel guilty about without having committed murder," I said.

Trent's eyes narrowed. "What do you mean?"

"If you'd been honest with the police at the time, you would have spared yourself a lot of grief. Mr. Collinsworth did not kill his wife."

He looked at me searchingly. "It *was* an accident, then?"

I dearly wished that were so. "Unknown. But he had no motive to kill her. Eunice had paid off his debts weeks before she died. I believe that was the guilt he struggled with."

"That's a relief," he murmured to himself, then gave me a sharp look. "But I'd never heard even a whisper about that. How do *you* know?" His eyes narrowed. "Are you really Miss Sinclair's cousin?"

"Of course I am." I stood. "I must be going."

He opened the door for me. "Why did you warn me about Reeves arrest? Aren't you worried I'll leave town?"

"I'm hardly in the position to stop you. Think of it as an opportunity to do the right thing. However, you may want to communicate with a certain young lady of your acquaintance before too long."

He bit his lip. "You're right, of course. Would you mind staying a few more minutes? I should write Miss Blakely a note.

If you would deliver it to her, that is?" His soft brown eyes were pleading.

How could I refuse?

I left him to his task while I went outside to inform Frank of the delay.

He frowned. "We risk running into that policeman while we wait here, playing cupid for a lovesick ne'er-do-well."

"It will take Jance a while to figure out the identities of Reeves and Trent from Shaw's journal. Besides, I believe Trent has potential. He'll be in a deal of trouble over this, but it might straighten him out for good."

"You always had a weakness for lost causes," he complained.

I flashed him a meaningful smile. "Not completely 'lost'."

His eyes softened and his voice grew tight. "Perhaps not."

Finally, Trent's missive in hand, we rattled out of there as quickly as we could without inviting attention.

I grabbed the arm rest as we made a sharp turn. "No sign of the police. You can slow down now."

He obligingly eased up on the reins. "Are we heading back to the cottage?"

"There's nothing else to be done here. Tell me, how's your investigation of Marsh coming along? I know it's only been one night so far."

"I've made a good start. He was at the Forty Steps late last night, so I had a chance to make his acquaintance and that of some others. He has an eye for the ladies, but you already knew that. He flirted shamelessly with the maids who came to sneak a cigarette. Most of the girls giggled and answered in kind, though one rebuffed him outright. Collinsworth's parlor maid, Marta. She turned right back the way she came when he addressed her."

"I've met her." At least the girl had good sense along with a pretty face. "What about the wealthy women in town?"

"He certainly didn't volunteer any names, but I noticed the expensive watch and signet ring you mentioned before. He was rather cagey about how he'd come by them. His employer isn't known to be so generous. I suspect he has—or had—a patroness of sorts."

Of sorts. I bit back a sigh. "If Marsh did have an affair with Eunice, I don't know how you can get him to admit it. At best, Bancroft would dismiss him on the spot. At worst, it could make him complicit in her death. He's too shrewd to risk that."

He gave me a sharp look. "That doesn't sound like you, Pen. You're not giving up, are you?"

I rubbed my temples. "Not at all. But we don't have much time. I wish the wedding had been postponed as Bridget suggested." I gave him a rueful look. "Having one's mother as a client is what makes this all so complicated."

He barked out a laugh. "Family—there's no avoiding them, is there? Always making a muddle of our lives."

No truer word was ever spoken.

"I have an idea to loosen Marsh's tongue," Frank went on. "But you're not going to like it." He hesitated.

"Yes?"

"I've learned the fellow has a fondness for French brandy. If a bottle from Lord Ashton's cellar can be spared, I thought I'd invite him to share it with me when he's free. Tomorrow night, maybe. I'll propose the idea when I see him tonight."

I scowled. "You're right. I don't like it." Frank's unquenchable thirst for spirits had been disastrous for our marriage, and nearly cost him his position at the agency.

Frank moved his hand from the reins briefly to cover my own. "Don't worry, Pen. I've worked too hard these last few years to return to my old ways." His voice took on a jesting tone. "I only hope your father can stand the thought of me pouring away expensive brandy."

I bit my lip. "Are you sure you can manage? Simply being around the stuff, the odor, having a full glass of it in your hand…it's a strong temptation."

We were pulling up to the Ashtons' cottage. Frank came around and handed me down. He leaned in to whisper, "If I can get something from Marsh, the risk will be worth it." His eyes softened. "And I feel I have something to prove to you as well."

Grace Collinsworth and Bridget stepped out of the house just then, deep in conversation. Since only my parents and Cassie knew Frank was my husband, it would look odd to see the family chauffeur lingering over my hand. I pulled away. Grace glanced at us with a speculative look.

Mercy. The last thing I needed was that sort of conjecture to complicate things.

"Oh, Pen, I'm so glad you're back," Bridget said. "Have you heard? The police are looking for Donald Reeves."

"*Looking* for him?" I glanced back at Frank. He gave a slight nod and circled around back toward the kitchen, no doubt to learn more.

"That's right." She glanced curiously at Frank's retreating form before turning back to me, her eyes troubled. "Reg is accompanying the policeman to Trent's house to inquire."

Grace frowned. "I've rarely seen my brother so upset. He wouldn't tell us what the police want of Reeves."

"This isn't because of the man who died, is it?" Bridget asked.

I was spared an answer by Grace rushing in with, "What nonsense! Reeves is a gentleman, and this fellow—from what I hear—was decidedly *not*. God rest his soul," she added virtuously.

"I suppose you're right," Bridget said. "We should go before it gets late." Upon my inquiring expression, she added, "Grace found a lace fan of her mother's she wants to show me, back at the house."

"You're welcome to come along with us," Grace offered.

As tempting as that was—after all, I wanted an opportunity to go through Collinsworth's dresser for a look at his cufflinks, just to tidy up loose ends—I shook my head. "I have something to take care of. Have you asked Cassie?"

"I haven't seen her," Bridget said. "I would have asked Rebecca but she's waiting for Trent. He's supposed to take her for a scenic drive. I hope the police visit doesn't delay him. She'd be devastated."

I grimaced as I reached for the door handle. Rebecca Blakely was my next task, and the news was more devastating than a missed outing.

CHAPTER 19

$\mathcal{I}$ found Miss Blakely in the front parlor seated by the window, delicate hands clasping a rosette-trimmed straw bonnet in her lap. There was no doubt she was watching for Trent's arrival.

"Miss Blakely, can I speak with you?"

The girl looked up in surprise. Not that I could blame her— we'd done little more than exchange meaningless pleasantries this entire week. "I'm afraid I'm expecting someone any minute, Miss Hamilton."

"Mr. Trent, you mean?" I shut the door and fished in my reticule for the sealed envelope. "You'll want to read this. It's from him."

With a puzzled frown, she tore it open.

I paced to the other end of the room and examined the clock on the mantel as she read.

"M-Miss Hamilton?"

I turned around. The young lady's usual rosy-pink complexion had drained to a grayish pallor.

"Are you ill?" I came over to sit beside her. "Shall I ring for smelling salts?"

"No, no—I'll be all right." She took a deep, gulping breath. "This is horrible. Will they really…arrest him?"

"It's hard to say. Certainly the police have questions. There will be uncomfortable times ahead for him in the public eye, even if he doesn't face criminal charges."

She flinched. Mother was right—I'm rather blunt at the worst times.

After a few minutes of sniffling on her part and ineffectual murmurs of sympathy on mine, I left her to her misery and went looking for my mother. She was my client, after all. I had a report to make.

I found her and Cassie in the rose garden with the gardener's lad, a skinny youth too tall for his britches with a sharp adam's apple that bobbed along his neck when he swallowed nervously, which was often.

"Be sure to snip enough for Miss Blakely's bouquet as well," Mother was saying, "but wait until late in the day on Friday. We want the blooms as fresh as possible."

Cassie murmured in agreement as she bent over a yellow rose to inhale its scent.

The fellow twisted his cap in his hands. I could tell he wanted to put it back on in the full sun, but didn't dare in Mother's presence. "Ya want me to take off the thorns, ma'am?"

Mother fixed him with a stern eye that made him squirm. "This is for a wedding, young man. What do you think?"

With a bow and a stammer under his breath, he excused himself.

Mother glanced my way. "Ah, Penelope, I need you to help Cassie snip lengths of ribbon and"—

I cut across whatever tedium she had planned. "I've made progress in the case. I'm here to give you my report."

Cassie sucked in a breath, but Mother confined her response to a raised eyebrow.

I took that as permission to continue. "It was Collinsworth's friend Trent who sent the anonymous note." I explained Trent's lie and his growing concern about Collinsworth's guilt.

Cassie's eyes widened. "Does that mean Bridget's fiancé *did* kill his first wife?"

"No. Trent mistakenly assumed Collinsworth still needed money to wipe out a slew of gambling debts."

"Gambling?" Mother echoed.

I told them what Johnny Shaw had found out about Collinsworth's debts and when they'd been paid. "I'm confident Collinsworth did not kill his wife, though I still can't say whether it really was an accident." I gave Mother a pointed look. "But for Bridget's sake, you'll want Collinsworth's reassurance that his gambling days are over and done."

Mother's mouth set in a grim line. "I'll speak to your father about it now. Excuse me."

We watched her cross the lawn, the set of her shoulders rigid.

"She didn't even thank you," Cassie said.

I patted her hand. "I don't know if I could have handled that, dear."

Thursday, June 23rd

I was back in the rose garden the next morning—this time with Bridget, who planned to surprise Grace with a corsage of salmon-tinted roses to match her dress on Saturday—when I observed the heart-sinking approach of a barrel-chested man in a navy-blue tunic uniform. Officer Jance. He clutched my abandoned straw hat.

He barely inclined his head in Bridget's direction as he eyed me. "I've caught up to you at last, Miss Hamilton." He held out the hat. "Yours, I believe?"

Bridget frowned in confusion as I wordlessly accepted it.

He glanced around appreciatively. "I haven't much opportunity to tour a rose garden as extensive as this one. Would you mind showing me around while we talk?"

It wasn't a request, of course. "Very well, sir." I passed the hat to Bridget. "Will you excuse us, dear? And put this on my dresser, if you don't mind."

"Of course." With one last, puzzled glance over her shoulder, Bridget left us.

Jance got right to the point as soon as she was out of earshot. "What were you doing in Mr. Shaw's room at Ocean House?"

I settled upon the details of what I would say as we turned down a gravel path toward a bed of Lady Ashton's heirloom roses. "I was helping Mr. Wynch," I said finally. "I'm aware he's a Pinkerton."

Jance stopped short. He put up a hand as if to scratch his graying mutton-chop whiskers, seemed to think better of it, and tugged at his collar instead. "Helping Wynch? With what?"

"With determining who Shaw was investigating, in case it was connected to his death."

The policeman scowled. "Wynch's interference is bad enough, but why would a gently born lady such as yourself be helping the likes of a detective?"

I had an answer ready for him, in the form of a blush and a stammer. "W-well, you-you know, sir, Mr. Wynch is rather…I mean, he-he's rather handsome. I was happy to help."

Jance relaxed, chuckling as he mopped his brow with his kerchief in the morning warmth. Here, at last, was a feminine motivation he could understand. "Sweet on 'im, eh? Enough to jump out a window?—you must have it real bad."

I assumed a wounded expression. "I would appreciate you keeping that particular escapade to yourself."

His eyes softened with a paternal gleam. "All right, then, your secret's safe. I suppose no real damage is done, as long as you don't start gossiping about what you read in the dead man's journal."

I swallowed a retort. *Land sakes*, he sorely tested my patience.

We continued our stroll to the next row—Lady Ashton's pink varieties.

He stopped to cradle a bloom, his large grip surprisingly gentle. "Tell me, miss, how much of the book *did* you read before I got there?"

"The last few pages. Mr. Wynch had hoped there might be a clue as to what Shaw was doing at the abandoned barn that night. You no doubt read it yourself—he was supposed to meet someone."

"Referred to him only as 'new client.'" He scowled. "No help there."

I again thanked Providence that Shaw had kept his word about not mentioning me by name. It would have been the height of absurdity to have to fend off suspicion of doing away with the poor fellow. "I learned from the pages that Shaw was working on a check-forging case and had discovered the culprit. Have you made any arrests in that regard? That's why you enlisted Mr. Collinsworth's assistance yesterday, I expect?"

He gave a grudging nod. "Two arrests so far."

"Tompkins and Reeves?"

He shot me a look. "How did you know?"

I shrugged. "Word gets around. What about Reeves friend, Mr. Trent?"

"He's at the station for another round of questioning. Nothing's been decided about him yet. Funny thing about Shaw's last entry," Jance went on, with a sharp look in my direction, "he'd written that he hadn't found the canceled checks, and yet there they were, sitting right on top of the book. Providential, I'd say. We would not have known to interview Mr. Matthews. He's the one who pointed us toward Reeves and Tompkins."

"Providential, indeed," I said, keeping my expression neutral. "Perhaps he'd found them after he wrote the entry, and had no time to update it."

"I suppose," he conceded.

"Who do you believe killed Shaw—Tompkins or Reeves?"

He stepped back from the rose. "It's best you stay out of it from here on, miss. You've meddled enough. This is a dangerous business. Leave it to those of us trained in catching criminals."

"Shaw's last log entry," I blithely meddled on, "mentioned that a man followed him earlier that day, just as he was concluding his check-forging case. It's not so very great a leap to extrapolate a connection between the two."

"I'm aware of that," he retorted.

"Have Tompkins and Reeves been able to account for their whereabouts the night Shaw was killed? Even Trent, for that matter, as he was mixed up in the scheme," I added. Though Maxwell Trent possessed some redeeming qualities, his role merited consideration. Reeves' influence upon him was considerable.

Jance pulled out his kerchief again and irritably dabbed at his neck. "Tompkins is not a suspect in Shaw's murder. He accompanied Bennett on an overnight sail to Nantucket and didn't return until Wednesday afternoon. Trent and Reeves corroborate each other."

Trent was up to his old behaviors, it seemed—first lying for Collinsworth and now Reeves. Did the man never learn? Just when I thought he was reformed...I shook my head in disgust. "You must know that doesn't count for much. Did the proprietress of Ocean House tell you of the other visitor asking for Shaw's room? A man with reddish-brown, wavy hair. Donald Reeves matches the description."

Jance sighed. "Reeves is denying everything at the moment, though that will change, I'm sure, once we get Trent to tell us what he knows. I plan to have the lady from Ocean House take a look at Reeves, but his reason for trying to get into the room is as plain as the nose on your face, begging your pardon. Naturally, he would want to make off with evidence against him in the check-forging scheme. But that doesn't mean he killed the detective. Besides, how would he know Shaw was going to be at the barn? He couldn't have followed him that night. Shaw would have taken extra precautions to be sure of that."

I gritted my teeth. My promise of silence to Mother meant I was in no position to tell Jance about my arranged meeting with Shaw—including who had learned of it in advance and might have shared it.

"How would Reeves have known it was safe to search Shaw's room unless he already knew he was dead?" I asked instead. "It was mere hours after the body was found. I assume you didn't make the dead man's identity widely known so early in your investigation."

Jance raised a shaggy eyebrow in surprise. "I did not. Only Wynch and a few men in the department knew."

"You've no doubt searched Reeves home for evidence of the check-forging scheme by now, but have you examined his personal effects? You might find the mate to the cufflink we found in the barn. Or telltale signs on an article of clothing— dirt or bloodstains he cannot account for."

A mix of conflicting emotions—grudging interest, irritation, and defensiveness—crossed his features. My point was taken, though he wouldn't admit it.

"Lord save me from ghoulish females," he muttered. He fixed me with a stern eye. "I'd avoid keeping company with Wynch in the future if I were you, Miss Hamilton. He's a poor influence on a lady of your station. I'm sure your family would agree." He gave a curt bow. "Now, if you'll excuse me."

I watched him hurry away. From the determined set of his shoulders, he appeared to be a man on a mission. I dearly hoped he was headed for Reeves' wardrobe.

CHAPTER 20

*T*hat evening, Mother, Cassie and I settled in the library for an after-dinner game of cards. Bridget was closeted upstairs with Miss Blakely. She was undoubtedly of more comfort than I'd managed to be.

The doorbell rang, and Mother cocked her head. "That will be Reg. It's just as well Bridget is occupied while he and your father have a talk."

An awkward conversation, to be sure, with Papa trying to establish that Collinsworth's gambling days were behind him.

The parlor maid tapped on the open door. "Mrs. Hamilton? Miss Collinsworth, ma'am." She stepped aside to allow the lady to pass.

Cassie and I exchanged a glance. Grace Collinsworth? Papa's request had been for her brother alone.

Mother gave a calm nod, as if she wasn't surprised at all. "Of course. Have tea and cakes brought in, if you please."

The girl withdrew.

"Grace, an unexpected pleasure." Mother gestured to the settee. "Please, be comfortable."

Grace Collinsworth was attired in an elegant, off-the-shoulder dinner frock of bronze silk which complimented her rich brown hair and creamy complexion. At the moment, however, her cheeks were flushed with agitation. She perched stiffly upon the edge of the settee and fixed my mother with an icy glare. "Why has Reg been summoned here by your husband, Mrs. Hamilton?" Her voice bristled with indignation. "Yesterday was trying enough for him, helping the police chase around Newport after Mr. Reeves"—she broke off as the maid entered with the tea tray. No one spoke as the girl arranged the items within Mother's convenient reach, gave a bob, and closed the door behind her.

Mother poured the tea with a steady hand, though I could see the strain in her clenched jaw. And no wonder. Here we were, less than two days before the wedding, with the best man facing police questioning and possible arrest, the lady of honor upstairs crying her eyes out over that fact, and the husband-to-be currently being taken to task by the bride's surrogate father regarding his reckless gaming habits.

Mother set down the teapot before answering. "Regarding Mr. Reeves, it is a sad state of affairs, to be sure. I do regret it was necessary to disturb your brother under such circumstances. Curtis simply wishes a private discussion with him. I had not anticipated you would become involved."

"Well, he *is* my brother," Grace snapped.

"And a grown man," Cassie pointed out. I was sitting beside her and caught the smirk as she lifted the cup to her lips.

"What do you want of Reg?" Grace asked impatiently.

Mother plucked a sugar cube from the bowl. "Let us just say that information of a concerning nature has come to light."

Grace's eyes narrowed. "What 'concerning information?'"

Mother gave a thin smile. "We should let the men to handle it. It needn't worry us." She picked up a plate. "Would you care for a madeleine, Miss Collinsworth?"

Apparently madeleines were an insufficient peace offering. Grace abruptly stood. "I know what you are about. You think my brother isn't good enough for your precious Bridget, so you hired a private detective to pry into his affairs."

Private detective. My heart raced. How could she have known?

"What on earth do you mean?" Mother's best peremptory voice is ordinarily sufficient to quell any insubordination, but Grace seemed immune.

"That man—Wynch. He's not really your driver." She folded her arms. "He's a Pinkerton. Reg told me so."

"Really?" Mother's delicate brows arched as far as they could climb up her forehead. "This is the first I have heard of it. What makes your brother believe something so outlandish, poor dear?"

I exchanged a glance with Cassie, whose twitching lips no doubt matched my own. Mother was good. Very, very good.

"W-well, I—I," Grace stammered. She drew a breath. "The policeman told him, when he asked Reg for help in finding Reeves. This is intolerable, Mrs. Hamilton."

Unease pricked my spine. I stared into my teacup. With the Collinsworths aware of Frank's true identity, in no time at all it would become common knowledge among the servants—and Marsh. Frank would have to abandon the scheme to ply Marsh with brandy tonight. I should warn him right away. But what then? How would we find out what really happened to Eunice Collinsworth?

"Pen," Cassie murmured.

"Hmm?" I looked up to see that both Grace and Mother had left the parlor. It was just the two of us. "Oh, sorry. I was preoccupied."

Cassie moved over to sit beside me. "That was awkward. Quite the protective sister, isn't she?"

"Indeed. She's gone home, I assume?"

"Yes. And your mother retired early with a headache."

"I feel one coming on myself." I stood. "Excuse me, dear. I believe some air will do me good."

As it was barely nine-o'clock—Frank's meeting with Marsh wouldn't be until later—I tried the cottage where Frank was bunking with the gardener and his son.

Frank answered the door, shirtsleeves rolled up, a half-smoked cigarette in his hand. "Pen! Come in, come in." He opened the door wider.

I stepped in cautiously. "You're alone?"

He nodded. "The gardener and his lad are out at a lodge meeting. They're staying in town with family for the night."

"Good. I need to talk with you."

He led the way to the tiny galley kitchen, where a couple of stools were positioned in front of the counter to form a rough eating space. The surface was littered with a crumpled cigarette pack, a coffee cup, a pen, and his logbook, open to a partially written page. My heart tugged with the homely familiarity of it all. I remembered many a time when Frank and I had our notes sprawled across the kitchen table, drinking coffee to keep us going as we discussed a case late into the night.

"I was just catching up on my entries," he explained, following my glance.

"I'm sorry to interrupt you. I have disturbing news."

He pulled out a stool and brushed it off. "Sit. Tell me." He took the other one and leaned in attentively.

"In the course of his inquiry, Officer Jance has revealed to Reg Collinsworth that you're a Pinkerton. Reg then told his sister, who's indignant that we would hire a detective to investigate her precious brother."

"Is she, now?" He pursed his lips as he thought. "Why did she assume I was looking into her brother? After all, Reeves has just been arrested in a check-forging scheme. Wouldn't that be the natural assumption to make? I never told Jance what case I was working on."

"Good point." I could always rely upon Frank's perspective.

"Perhaps she was suspicious of her brother's role in his wife's death?" Erroneously so, as I'd discovered from reading Shaw's last entry.

Unless—I felt a chill. Unless Collinsworth's motive hadn't been a financial one at all. What if he'd just discovered his wife had a lover? Would that have pricked his pride, or enraged him enough to push her off a cliff?

"Well, Trent was worried enough to send that anonymous note to your mother," he said, breaking into my thoughts.

"And Mother then pulled me into it."

"Grace doesn't know about the note?"

"No."

"So she doesn't know you've been investigating her brother?" he asked.

"She doesn't suspect I'm a Pinkerton, if that's what you mean. Perhaps Lady Ashton's gossip never reached her ears. What concerns me now is word of your true identity circulating below-stairs. If Grace is as voluble at home as she was here, the servants will pick it up. It could get back to Marsh. We still don't know if he's a threat or not."

His eyes softened and he clasped my hand in his strong, warm ones. "Pen—you *do* still care about me."

I let my hand rest there for a bare moment before gently withdrawing it. "Someone has to," I answered lightly. "It may as well be me."

To give him credit, he didn't press the point. Checking his watch, he said, "Marsh and I have arranged to meet back here for that drink, once his employer has retired for the night. That's just a few hours from now. It's highly doubtful he would have heard any gossip by then." He pointed to a rough-hewn pine cupboard in the corner. "Your father has already supplied me with the brandy."

I frowned. "And you believe you can avoid drinking any without Marsh noticing?"

"If all goes according to plan, we'll be out on the porch

enjoying it in the night air." He grinned. "The climbing roses might be the worse for wear afterward."

I still didn't like it. "All may not go according to plan."

"I can take care of myself. Trust me, Pen." He stood, and before I knew what he was about, he'd gathered me into his arms.

I circled my arms around his neck as the once-familiar sensations returned—his firm hand gently cradling the back of my neck, the soft brush of his whiskers against my cheek, his warm lips pressed against mine. I was immersed in the smoky, outdoor scent of him, and couldn't tell if the rapid heartbeat I felt was his or my own. Frank knew how to kiss me in a way no man ever would, and my fickle composure left me to fend for myself.

"I've wanted to do that for a long time," he finally murmured into my hair.

I drew a deep, ragged breath and stepped back, hoping my knees would keep me steady. "Frank—we still cannot...live together. That hasn't changed."

He dropped his hands. "But I love you. And I know you love me. You can't deny it."

"I don't deny it. I do love you."

He blew out a long, slow sigh. That must have been weighing on him these past few years.

"It's not as simple as that," I went on. "The possibility may lay in our future. I don't know. I can only tell you that, right now, I'm not prepared to take that step."

"I know I hurt you—in many ways." His voice was subdued. "I regret that deeply."

"What's done is done. But"—I expelled a breath and fixed him with a mock-stern gaze—"if you want to remain in my good graces, you'll be careful tonight."

He spread his hands in a gesture of innocence. "Careful? I'm always careful."

CHAPTER 21

Friday, June 24th

*A*ll through breakfast my eyes kept straying to the door of the dining room, half-expecting word from Frank. He wouldn't appear in person to speak with me, of course, as that would attract notice, but I'd hoped he'd send a note.

Perhaps he hadn't been successful in learning anything of value. Marsh might not be the promising lead we'd thought.

Another, more disturbing possibility struck me. What if Frank had drunk himself into a stupor and was still sleeping it off?

Trust me, Pen.

Easier said than done. Last night's kiss had not magically restored the man I'd first married.

My train of thought was interrupted when Papa stepped into the room, alone.

"Where's Mother?" I asked.

"Upstairs with a headache."

"Still? Will she be all right?" It must be a formidable one to keep her abed the day before Bridget's wedding with so much left to be done.

He poured himself a cup of coffee and sat across from me. "I expect so. This one was brought on by that Collinsworth woman."

"I'm surprised Mother would allow Grace to trouble her for very long."

"In the light of morning, other worries have surfaced," he said. "Concern over our family's reputation, for one. How will it look if it becomes widely known we had Bridget's future husband investigated? The other concern is for Bridget herself...." His voice trailed off.

I looked up, startled. "Didn't Mother tell you what I discovered? Collinsworth had no financial motive to kill his first wife."

Even as I said it, the nagging possibility of another, more personal motive lingered at the edge of my mind.

He waved a placating hand in my direction. "She told me. That's not what worries me."

"Then what—his gambling?"

"Surprising about that—the fellow confessed all to me before I could even confront him with what you'd discovered."

"You didn't reveal my role in this, I hope?"

"Never fear, he has no idea of the source. I kept that to myself."

"He and his sister believe your information came from Frank," I said.

"Collinsworth never said a word about that. He may have been too preoccupied with contrition. He swore to me he hasn't gambled since his wife's death."

"You believe him?"

Papa's smile was tight-lipped. "Now that I know what I'm looking for, it's easy enough to check. I've already sent out inquiries this morning. I should hear within a few hours."

"Did you send Frank to town with the message?" That would explain his silence.

"No, the Mullins' boy took it." He squinted at me in curiosity. "Why do you ask?"

"Never mind. What concerns you about Bridget marrying Collinsworth, then?"

"Having Grace Collinsworth as her sister-in-law, that's what," he retorted. "A more intrusive, protective in-law-to-be I have yet to meet. And remember, I had your mother's mama to deal with back in the day, God rest her soul."

"Grace *is* rather like a mother to Collinsworth," I mused. "If I remember their family history, she was in her twenties and he was just a boy when they were orphaned. Didn't she have the care of him?" That would explain her protective impulses.

"Indeed—and turned away several marriage prospects as a result, I've heard. A shame. If she were married now, she wouldn't be intruding into the affairs of the prospective newlyweds."

"I'm sure Bridget can stand up for herself."

Papa distractedly groped in his pockets, then gave it up with a sigh and reached for a teacup instead. "It's been a difficult week," he muttered.

"Any word on whether Mr. Trent has been arrested?"

"Not to my knowledge. Reg sent a note this morning saying he's heading to the police station to see what he can find out. A sad state of affairs, with the wedding tomorrow."

"What about postponing it?"

"I don't see how we could stop it now, even if we wanted to. Guests are arriving by train tonight and tomorrow morning." He scowled at his eggs.

I rested a hand on his shoulder as I got up to leave. "Cheer up, Papa. All one really needs for a wedding are a bride, a groom, and a minister."

I stepped outside to what looked to be a gloomy day. It wasn't raining yet, but the sky was getting grayer by the minute and the wind was kicking up. I made my way to the gardener's cottage to check on Frank.

Before knocking upon the door, I circled around to the side of the porch, looking for signs that Frank and Marsh had indeed spent time there last night. My search was rewarded with two cigar stubs and a few burnt matches beneath the wood bench. I surveyed the climbing rose shrub that sprawled along the baluster. After a quick look over my shoulder to be sure I was unobserved, I crouched at the base of the shrub and sniffed. The odor of brandy, mixed with the scent of roses and warming soil, wafted up.

I blew out a deep breath. He'd kept his word.

A glint among the stems caught my eye. Ah, the bottle.

I was carefully reaching through the thorny vegetation to grasp it when I heard the front door open. I hastily straightened, scratching my forearm in the process.

The gardener stepped out, followed by his son. The gardener squinted at me in curiosity. "Lose somethin', miss?"

"No, no, I'm fine. Just admiring your roses."

Of course the blooms weren't close to the ground where I'd been squatting, but the man seemed to have the good sense not to comment upon the fact and settled for a grunt.

"I came to speak with the driver," I explained. "Wynch, I believe? I wish to go into town today. Is he in?"

"Sorry, miss, haven't seen 'im."

"Well, I suppose I'll keep looking. Thank you."

He and the boy left, heading for the gardener's shed.

Once they were out of sight, I tried the door. Unlocked. I slipped in.

There were two bedrooms—the gardener's and his son's. Judging by the stack of neatly folded blankets, bed linens, and pillow at the end of a small sofa in the living room, Frank had been making do with makeshift sleeping arrangements. I recognized his valise, too, tucked in the corner. I felt for the brush in his shaving kit. Dry. Either he hadn't shaved this morning, or hadn't spent the night here at all. Where was he?

I checked the carriage house next. No sign of him. I was about to make a complete circuit of the grounds when I spotted Cassie coming along the path from the shore.

"Ah, Pen!" she said brightly, clutching her hat as a stiff breeze kicked up. "Out for a walk?"

"Looking for Frank, actually. You haven't seen him?"

"No, sorry. But I wouldn't go far, dear," she warned. "There's a storm coming."

"It doesn't look like much. I'll risk a wetting."

"It may become worse than that. Here within the tree line it's hard to tell. There's a better view along the Walk—clouds are rolling in, and the water's getting choppy out on the bay. Fishermen are pulling up their nets."

"No matter. I have to go." Every instinct told me Frank was in trouble.

Cassie gave me a long, probing look. "Well, then, I'm coming with you. But let's fetch raincoats first."

Properly equipped, we finished our tour of the grounds, even stopping by the kitchen. No sign of him, and he hadn't been seen all morning.

"Do you mind if we head back along the Cliff Walk to look?" I asked.

Cassie blinked in surprise. "You're profoundly worried about him. Why?"

As we took the path that connected to the Walk, I told her about Frank's scheme to elicit more information from Joe Marsh.

She clucked her tongue. "Frank and French brandy? No wonder you're worried."

"I wasn't thrilled with the idea, believe me. But no better alternative presented itself."

"Which way?" she asked, as the path from the house intersected with the Walk.

"Let's head south, towards Rosecliff. That's Mr. Bancroft's place."

"You think Frank kept Marsh under observation after he left?" Cassie asked.

"Possibly."

The wind whipped our skirts and blew sea spray in our faces as we took the path. Cassie was right—it did look to be a bigger storm than I'd first thought. Dark clouds piled atop each other against a now steel-gray sky. A number of men were scattered along the shore, pulling in boats and coiling rope.

Rosecliff came into view. I hesitated. Should we pay a call upon Bancroft as a pretext to talk to Marsh?

Cassie nearly bumped into me as I stopped in the path. "We'd better turn back," she said. "We'll have a downpour any minute."

I surveyed our surroundings. "All right, but I'm going to continue past the cottage, toward the Forty Steps—" I broke off. In the gloom I'd nearly missed the dark, huddled form that lay among the rocks below. It was a man, motionless.

"Cassie." I tried to keep the quaver from my voice. "Go to Bancroft's and get help. Quickly."

Without waiting for an answer, I scrambled down the steep slope, skidding on loose rock and putting out my hands to control my descent. A sob plucked at my throat. *Please, no.*

I somehow got down to the shore without breaking my neck and scrambled over to the form. It was Frank. He was lying on his side, one leg bent under him at an odd angle and the back of his head matted with what must be blood. His clothes were damp. I leaned in close. His clothes smelled of briny water and blood and a hint of cigar. "Frank," I murmured in his ear.

He didn't stir. I probed the cold, clammy skin of his neck, searching for a heartbeat.

To my enormous relief, I felt a flutter under my fingertips and then his breath upon my cheek. *Thank heaven.*

I dare not move him from the damp rocks, so I had to settle for draping him with my raincoat.

Help arrived at last in the form of Bancroft and two other men—his stable hand and groundskeeper, as it turned out—carrying a makeshift stretcher. I wondered where Marsh was.

Sleeping off the brandy? I had some questions for him once Frank was taken care of.

"There's a head wound. And watch the leg," I said.

Bancroft stood beside me as his men gently lifted Frank onto the tarpaulin that had been lashed between two poles. "Your friend, Miss Leigh, has gone back to the cottage to inform your father of what has happened."

"And to have a doctor sent for, I assume," I said.

A troubled expression flicked in his deep-set eyes. "Mr. Wynch's condition will require more than our local country doctor can provide. He must be taken directly to the hospital. My driver is hitching up the cart now."

"You are very kind. May I go along?"

He shot me a puzzled glance.

Bancroft, of course, didn't know I was Frank's wife, so I could see why it appeared odd for me to be accompanying an injured male servant in my father's employ.

"At least until my father can get to the hospital," I added quickly. "It seems the considerate thing to do, under the circumstances."

"Of course. You can ride with the driver, if you don't mind sharing the front bench."

"I'll manage."

"All right, then. I must be getting back." He bowed over my hand. "Good luck to the fellow. I hope he recovers."

CHAPTER 22

$\mathcal{P}$apa joined me in the hospital waiting room a while later.

"Any word yet?" he asked, drawing up a chair.

"Nothing." With a quick glance at a family on the other side of the room, I leaned in and dropped my voice. "It was no accident, Papa. Someone tried to kill him."

He frowned. "I was afraid of that. He was still inquiring into Eunice's death, correct?"

"Yes, and what happened to him looks a lot like what happened to Eunice. It cannot be a coincidence. I don't know whether it was because he discovered something, or his true identity had become known. Thanks to Officer Jance and the Collinsworths," I added sharply.

He put his hand over mine. "Don't be bitter, Pen. Reg and his sister meant no harm. Frank knew the risks."

A weary-looking, gray-haired gentleman in steel-rimmed spectacles and a lumpy brown jacket stepped into the room. He squinted at Papa. "Mr. Hamilton?" We followed him out to the stairwell for privacy.

"I'm Doctor Latz." He shook hands with my father. "You are Mr. Wynch's employer, sir?"

Papa made a face. "In a manner of speaking. But I want you to do everything you can to save him. I'll take care of the expense."

"Rest assured we are indeed doing just that. We've set the leg, put his dislocated shoulder back into place, and the cracked ribs will heal, given time." He scowled. "However, I don't know if he has time. His head injury is quite serious. He's still unconscious. Is there any family we can contact?"

Papa glanced at me and I gave a slight nod. I didn't care who knew, now. "This is his wife," he said.

The doctor's eyes softened. "I'm sorry to be the bearer of bad news, ma'am."

I swallowed. "May I see him?"

"Of course." He turned to lead the way.

Papa touched my arm. "I'll wait here. Take all the time you need."

Because of the extent of his injuries, Frank was in a private room rather than one of the wards. A white-aproned attendant sat in a chair beside the bed.

She got up at our approach. "His respiration is regular, doctor, and his pulse is steady now."

"Well, that's something." The doctor turned to me. "We'll give you some time alone with him, Mrs. Wynch."

I approached the bed, ignoring everything else but the sight of him. He looked so fragile, his head swathed in bandages, arm in a sling, leg immobilized. Scrapes adorned one whiskered cheek.

I sat with him for a while, holding his limp hand, murmuring to him. He didn't wake, but his breathing was easy. I wasn't sure whether or not to feel hopeful.

What I did know was that I had to learn who was responsible. And my first step was to talk to Marsh.

I got up and leaned over to gently kiss my husband on the brow, just below the bandage. "Frank," I whispered, "I have to leave you now. I need to find out who did this. But I am not saying goodbye, you hear me? You promised me you would take care of yourself. I ex-expect you to keep your promise." I swiped my damp cheeks with the back of my hand as I left the room.

Papa frowned when I told him my intent. "You shouldn't go gallivanting after clues. Your place is beside your husband in his final moments."

"I rarely gallivant," I retorted, "and I'm a better judge of my place. That's the sort of comment I'd expect from Mother."

His jaw clenched. "I suppose."

"Frank would be the first person to support my inquiry. There's nothing more I can do here. Can you drop me off at George Bancroft's cottage on your way home?"

Papa drew breath to answer just as the waiting room door opened. To my astonishment, Gordon Bennett walked in. He looked exceptionally dapper today, attired in a light-gray seersucker suit with matching gray cravat and white straw boater. I wondered if he'd hired a new valet already. Of course, the man was probably capable of dressing himself. Just not able to spot a check-forger in his midst.

He headed straight for us, his brows creased in a determined expression.

I was in no mood to deal with Bennett right now.

"Let's go, Papa." I called over my shoulder. I walked briskly past the open-mouthed Bennett and kept going until I'd gained the sidewalk.

It soon became evident my stratagem for ignoring the newspaper mogul was not going to work, however. He and Papa, deep in conversation, followed me out at a more leisurely pace. As Papa was my ride back, I had to wait for them to catch up to me. To add insult to injury, it was beginning to drizzle.

"Miss Hamilton." Bennett bowed over my gloved hand but kept his frost-blue eyes upon me all the while.

I quickly withdrew my hand. "Have you come to gloat over

figuring out I'm a Pinkerton? I cannot admire your methods, sir. You managed to alarm my employer with spurious claims such that he was obliged to send another detective, the one currently unconscious at the hospital."

He started to speak, but I overrode him, my anger and frustration taking a caustic edge. "Or have you come to explain how you overlooked an uncomfortable truth at your own door, in the form of your check-forging valet?"

He winced. "I've come to apologize," he said quietly. "I jumped to conclusions and acted where I should not have, all while missing the real malfeasance right under my nose." He grimaced. "Being duped is a unique experience for me."

And no doubt a humbling one. Out of the corner of my eye I saw Papa's lips twitch as he pulled up his collar against the drizzle.

"I would have paid a proper call upon you sooner," Bennett went on, "but after Tompkins' arrest I've been busy squelching rumors and speculation that could damage my reputation." He gripped his hat in his hands awkwardly. "Will your associate recover?"

"We don't know. It doesn't look...promising."

He gave me a speculative look. I expelled a breath and clamped down more firmly upon my elusive composure.

"Do you know who attacked him?" he asked.

At least the man wasn't offering empty platitudes, for which I was grateful. "I'm about to find out." I looked over at Papa, who cleared his throat.

"Mr. Bennett and I were talking. He can drive you to Rosecliff. That would give you two a chance to catch up on recent events. I should be getting back to your mother. I'm sure she's no end of worried about what's going on."

I gave a bitter smile. Mother didn't care a jot about Frank. For her, the issue at hand was how it would affect the wedding tomorrow.

"I'll take you anywhere you need to go, Miss Hamilton," Bennett said.

"All right." I gave him a stern look. "But *no* street racing."

His eyes widened in innocence. "Naturally."

The interchange was punctuated by a rumble of thunder in the distance, and he ran ahead to his conveyance to open the door for me.

I clasped Papa's hand briefly in goodbye before following.

"Be careful, Penelope!" Papa called.

The low-roofed carriage was made more comfortable with waterproof curtains pulled along the open sides to keep out most of the rain. Bennett was true to his word, keeping the horse to a brisk trot.

"I'm sorry your fellow Pinkerton—Wynch, is it?—is in such bad shape," he said.

"How did you find out so quickly about his injury?" I asked.

"A number of servants in the important households around here know I pay to learn about such things. One must keep in touch, you know."

"That didn't help you any with your own staff," I observed.

His hands tightened briefly on the reins, then relaxed. "It did not. Tompkins—not his real name, as it turns out—had a well-crafted set of false credentials." He made a noise of irritation in the back of his throat. "Fooled me completely. And here I was worried about that other man—Shaw?—who wasn't a thief, but a detective, just like you and Wynch."

"Not 'just like' us," I said defensively. "He was from a different agency. Such methods as he used are frowned upon by Mr. Pinkerton."

He barked a laugh as he briefly glanced my way. "*You* have never employed such tactics, Miss Hamilton?"

I hid my smirk by looking down at my gloved hands. "Not quite to such, *erm*, extremes. I assume it was the police who told you about Shaw? Did they tell you what happened to him?"

His jaw clenched. "Yes. Poor fellow. I wish you'd told me who he really was."

"I promised him I would not. It might have jeopardized his investigation. He didn't trust me fully as it was. Though he told me about Tompkins' role in the check-forging scheme, he didn't name the other men he'd had under surveillance, Reeves and Trent. No doubt because I am acquainted with them."

"So the day I saw you and Shaw when we docked"—

—"was when I first learned who he was and what he was up to, yes. I realized how it would appear when you saw us together, but I wasn't in the position to refute your suspicions."

"At least we have an understanding now." He slowed to allow a pony cart to cross in front of us. "So why are we going to see Bancroft?"

"*I* am going to speak with Bancroft's secretary, Marsh. You can drop me off."

Bennett waved a hand toward the road ahead, where the rain was pelting down now in sheets. "You can't walk back afterward in this."

"But I need to speak with Marsh alone. I believe he attacked Frank."

"All the more reason to accompany you," he retorted.

"I can take care of myself. Besides, I'll be speaking with him in Bancroft's well-staffed house, not on a lonely, cliff-side path in the dark."

He kept his eyes on the road in sulky silence. He obviously wasn't used to being thwarted.

"All right," he grumbled at last. "I'll wait in the carriage. Will that suffice?"

"Yes."

Bancroft's parlor maid showed me directly to his study, where the scholar was standing over several volumes spread out upon his desk.

"Miss Hamilton, sir." She bobbed a curtsy and withdrew.

He looked up at me over his spectacles. "Miss Hamilton, this is a surprise! How's your driver doing?" He gestured toward a chair and took a seat across from me.

"There's no change, though they've made him more comfortable."

He made a *tsk*-ing sound. "A sad affair."

"I was hoping you'd permit me to speak with your secretary, Mr. Marsh."

He frowned. "Oh? In what regard?"

"He may have useful information concerning what happened to Mr. Wynch. This wasn't an accident."

"Indeed? Why would someone wish to harm your driver?"

I clasped my gloved hands in my lap. Mother wasn't going to like this one bit, but we had no choice. "He's only been posing as our driver. Mr. Wynch is in fact a private detective, looking into a confidential matter for the family. However, word of his true identity had begun to circulate. I've been retracing the events of last night and I understand Marsh was with him for some period of time."

Bancroft stroked his full, white beard and surveyed me thoughtfully. "Assuming what you say to be true, how does a well-bred lady find herself conducting the inquiry?"

The agile intellect of George Bancroft served him well in far more areas than academia and public service.

I knew there was no prevaricating. I would have to tell him. Mother wasn't going to like that, either. "I'm also a private detective. Mr. Wynch and I have been working together."

He sat back at that.

I waited for the inevitable skepticism to follow, the comments I'd heard time and time again. *What is a woman doing in such a sordid business? One should not go about claiming to do man's work in an attempt to appear more important. Your marriage prospects are sure to suffer.*

But Bancroft said none of these. He looked at me steadily,

speculatively, as if trying to read the truth in my posture and face. Finally, he spoke. "Lady Ashton was right."

I never thought I'd be thankful to the gossipy woman for smoothing the way to such news. "My mother would never publicly acknowledge it, but yes, Lady Ashton was correct. Of course, one would wish she'd been more discreet. I do hope you will keep this confidential."

He waved a dismissive hand. "Naturally. It's not entirely Lady Ashton's fault, you know. I spend my winters in Washington and I'd heard something of it from Senator Cullom himself, though not the name of the lady detective. Cullom's an upstanding, hard-working public servant. For him to admire your work is high praise indeed." He went over and pulled the bell.

A maid entered within moments. "Sir?"

"Fetch Marsh right away."

"Yes, sir."

He resumed his seat after she closed the door behind her. "Why would Wynch keep company with my secretary? Was it connected to your investigation?"

"Frank has been cultivating Marsh's acquaintance these past few days. Last night, Frank's plan was to invite him back to his lodgings and ply him with brandy in order to loosen his tongue."

A frown creased Bancroft's high-domed forehead. "'Loosen his tongue'? Regarding what?"

Here I was, straying further into sensitive territory. Well, neck or nothing. "Whether he was having an affair with Eunice Collinsworth, and if he'd had a hand in her death, accidentally or otherwise."

"Marsh?"

"You gave me the idea, Mr. Bancroft. When we first met on the Walk, you confirmed my impression that your secretary was something of a ladies' man, and that he regularly spent late-night hours along the Walk, particularly by the Forty Steps. As you know from your own sad experience, that's where Eunice Collinsworth died."

"Many an idle servant spends time there."

I inclined my head in acknowledgment. "What struck me in particular, however, was your comment—'There was that one time when I wondered—but *him?*' That was after I'd speculated about Eunice going out to meet someone the night of her death."

Bancroft was silent, keeping his gaze fixed upon the fire in the hearth.

I glanced at the mantel clock. It seemed to be taking a while for Marsh to answer his employer's summons. "What 'one time' had you been referring to, sir?" I asked.

He met my eye then. "I saw something." His expression turned gloomy. "But I'm still not sure. I don't wish to speak out of turn."

"I won't publicly reveal anything sensitive unless it's absolutely necessary."

He sighed. "About a week before Eunice died, I was out on the Walk quite late at night—a bout of insomnia that I hoped some fresh air might cure. As I was rounding a bend in the path I heard Marsh's voice. Up ahead I saw a man and a woman, embracing."

"And it was Eunice? You saw her?"

"No." He grimaced. "They were in silhouette. But it was her height and form, and she had on that enormous, wide-brimmed hat that had been a favorite of hers. I'd seen her wear it on more than one occasion."

I remembered seeing it, too, at Collinsworth's house, in the music room. It had been part of the housekeeper's shrine to the deceased lady—the hat, shawl, and fan arranged upon the piano, beside the ever-present vase of flowers.

"Sir?" The maid stood in the doorway. "Mr. Marsh is gone."

Bancroft gave an annoyed grunt. "What do you mean,

gone? He was supposed to be working in the map room. He had no reason to go out."

The girl bit her lip. "Not gone *out*, sir, just...gone. The housekeeper checked his room when we couldn't find him. His valise is missing, and the drawers are empty. She found this and told me to show you right away." She held out a folded slip of paper.

By this point, Bancroft and I were both on our feet.

He took the note, read it through, and silently passed it to me.

Urgent matters require my attention. I must quit your employ. I regret the short notice. ~J.M.

Bancroft's expression was grim as he gave a curt nod to the maid. "All right, Anna. That will be all."

"Yes, sir." She closed the door behind her.

I met his eye. "You know what this means."

"You think he fled because he attacked Wynch?"

"That's looking likely, wouldn't you agree?"

"Perhaps. I have difficulty thinking him capable of it."

"When did you see him last?"

"This morning." He pursed his lips. "Just after—yes—it was just after I'd returned from directing my driver to take Wynch to the hospital. Marsh came downstairs, wondering what the commotion was about. I told him, of course, then reminded him he had notes of mine to transcribe. I've been working in my study since then. But if he's responsible, what made him flee this morning, instead of last night, immediately after committing the deed?"

"He didn't count on Frank surviving. But now he knows Frank could awaken and name him." I glanced at the mantel clock. Three hours had elapsed. Was there still a chance of catching him? "How would he have left—on foot?"

"Must have. The stable lad would have never released a horse to him without my permission."

"You're not far from Narragansett Avenue," I mused aloud. "He could have picked up a hansom there." I hurried to the door. "I'll check the train station."

"He's sure to be long gone," Bancroft called out.

I didn't trouble to reply as I headed down the hall, snatched up my coat, and ran out the front door.

Bennett came around to open the carriage door for me, as I was still sticking my arm through the sleeve of my coat and getting thoroughly drenched in the process. "Success?"

"Hardly," I retorted. "Marsh is gone. We may still be able to catch him if the weather has delayed his train. How quickly can you get us to the station?"

His pale-brown mustache curled in a grin. "Let's see, shall we?"

CHAPTER 23

There's a special Providence that watches over idiots, drunken men, and boys, as the saying goes, and thankfully Providence's watchfulness extended to lady detectives on this occasion. The rain was blinding, but Bennett drove through it at a stunning pace, weaving around slower vehicles and once nearly tipping us on a sharp curve. When we pulled up to the station, I had to consciously un-flex my fingers where they'd stiffened upon the seat handle in a viselike grip. I jumped out without waiting for Bennett, though I was sure he'd be right behind me.

I hurried up the steps to the platform as lightning lit the sky briefly—long enough to see a lone man, valise at his feet, standing under the shelter of an overhang.

A crack of thunder soon followed.

Bennett had caught up to me. "Is that Marsh?" He had to practically shout in my ear over the sounds of the storm and an approaching locomotive.

"Yes!" I shouted back.

Marsh was stepping forward to meet the train as we hurried toward him.

"Not so fast, my good fellow!" Bennett seized him by the

shoulders and, in an impressive wrestling move, pinned his arms behind his back.

Marsh's outraged expression quickly changed to dismay when he laid eyes on me. "Miss Hamilton! What-what's going on?"

I took charge of Marsh's valise. "You know exactly what this is about." After a glance at the porter, who'd just stepped down from a nearby railcar and looked us over quizzically, I said to Bennett, "We'd better get him inside the station."

Marsh tried to wriggle free, but Bennett held him fast. "You can walk there under your own power, or I can carry you," he said through gritted teeth. Marsh stopped struggling.

There are benefits to keeping company with a rich and famous man. One of them is that regular workaday fellows ask few questions and are quick to oblige. The stationmaster, agape at the sight of three dripping people—one of whom was the formidable Gordon Bennett—promptly turned over the use of his office when that man requested a place for a private conversation. Even hot tea and towels were provided for our comfort.

Marsh silently accepted both, eyeing us warily.

Bennett set aside his soaked jacket and gave a mock-bow in my direction. "He's all yours, Miss Hamilton."

Too restless to sit, I leaned against the stationmaster's desk and faced Marsh. "Why did you attack Frank Wynch?"

The man narrowed his eyes. "What a presumptuous question. And who are you to stop me from boarding my train? That's kidnapping, you know. I've a mind to call the police."

"You're certainly welcome to do so," I said easily, "but I doubt you will. The police will have some questions for *you*. You were the last person to see Mr. Wynch last night, and his supposed accident was a stone's throw from Rosecliff. You'd discovered he was a detective, had you not? He was investigating your role in Eunice Collinsworth's death. He must have gotten a bit too close to the truth, and so you tried to kill him."

Marsh rubbed his temples. Apparently even expensive

brandy leaves a lingering headache. He looked up in confusion. "Detective? Frank?"

I ignored his pathetic attempt at ignorance. "But you were too intoxicated to do a very good job of it. Frank survived. When you discovered he lived, you feared he would wake and name you as his attacker. So you tried to flee."

A puzzled expression remained firmly fixed upon his brow.

"And what else did you fear, Mr. Marsh?" I continued. "Would he have also named you as Eunice Collinsworth's murderer?"

That seemed to have sparked something. Marsh's eyes widened and he spread his hands in a placating gesture. "I swear, I didn't kill her."

"We'll get back to that. Tell me about last night."

"Frank invited me to share a bottle of brandy. We lingered over it and talked a long time." He smothered a groan. "I do regret drinking so much of it, though."

"What happened when you were done?"

"I couldn't manage the path to walk home, so Frank came along with me, propped me up. I don't remember all of it, but I seemed to have gotten back without mishap. Only a little the worse for wear." He rubbed his neck. "He's a decent fellow, even if he's a—what'd you say?—Pinkerton."

I frowned. Marsh was claiming—quite plausibly—that he'd been too inebriated to even return home under his own power. Attacking Frank in such a condition would have been impossible. "If you didn't try to kill Frank, why abruptly leave Bancroft's employ this morning?"

"To stay out of trouble," he mumbled, looking down at his hands.

Bennett and I exchanged a glance.

"What sort of trouble?" Bennett asked. His impish grin was so wide I caught a glimpse of tobacco-stained teeth beneath his capacious brown mustache. "Female trouble, maybe?"

I started. I hadn't thought of that. Could it be sheer coincidence that Marsh had fled just after Frank was discovered, and Marsh was in fact trying to avoid some amorous entanglement? Could he have gotten a servant with child—perhaps the Collinsworth maid, Marta? According to Frank, she refused to speak to Marsh when the servants congregated on the Forty Steps. Perhaps she was fearful of her condition….

I was so lost in thought I nearly missed what Marsh said in reply.

"Oh, she's *trouble* all right. I don't want to be next."

Wait a minute. "Next?" I echoed. "As in—the next victim?"

He nodded.

"Because you know too much?" I asked.

He shrugged but didn't answer.

"Know too much about what?" Bennett asked impatiently, turning to me.

The wisp of an idea was beginning to solidify. "Marsh knows too much about Eunice Collinsworth's death. He doesn't want to be hit over the head and pushed off a cliff, as were Frank and Eunice."

Bennett's eyes narrowed. "Wait—he said 'she's trouble.' You mean a *woman* is responsible for both incidents?"

"Exactly." More pieces were falling into place—Eunice's hat, easily borrowed by any female in the Collinsworth household and seen in silhouette during a romantic embrace; the Collinsworth house conveniently close to the Walk; the Collinsworth maid in a huff with Marsh, but not because she was the object of Marsh's attentions. No—she was jealous because her *mistress* was the recipient of them.

I felt confident about the latter as I observed the nervous secretary fiddling with the ring on his little finger that caught red glints in the light. A maid could not gift her lover with a ruby-encrusted signet ring, or the expensive watch on the gold chain at his vest.

But Grace Collinsworth could.

Even Eunice going out without a lantern the night she was

killed made sense now. If she'd grown suspicious of Grace's comings and goings and decided to follow her, she would have left the lantern behind so as not to give herself away.

And there was the night we'd stayed at the Collinsworth estate. I'd seen an unknown woman quietly slipping into the house in the early morning hours. She hadn't come from the direction of the seaside, as if on a walk, but farther back along the property. The dower house was in that direction, the place where Grace had first lived after Reg married Eunice. Closed up now, untenanted. Away from prying eyes.

"Mr. Marsh." I stepped closer and waited until he looked up. "Did you see Grace Collinsworth kill Eunice?"

I heard Bennett suck in his breath.

Marsh's gaze dropped to his hands.

"Look at me," I said in a steely voice. He reluctantly met my eye. "Did you see her do it?"

Marsh rubbed the back of his neck in a weary gesture. "No."

"But you did see Eunice that night, didn't you? You must tell us exactly what happened."

After an uneasy glance at Bennett, he took a ragged breath. "Grace and I met at our usual spot that night—below the Forty Steps and a little away from the path, where we couldn't be seen from above. We were deep in conversation—she was worried her sister-in-law was suspicious of us. Next thing we knew, there was Mrs. Collinsworth, heaping invectives on Grace. She seemed to blame her husband's gambling woes upon his sister's 'Jezebel nature.'" He grimaced. "Her words, not mine."

"What did you do?" Bennett asked.

"I feared the argument would attract attention. Even that early in the morning there might have been someone within earshot. I tried placating Mrs. Collinsworth, but when that didn't work, I left them to sort it out."

"When you heard about Eunice's death later," I said, "didn't you wonder if Grace was responsible?"

"I asked her, once. 'Accidents happen,' she said." He pulled out his gold watch and opened it. "She gave me this, and told me not to worry about it."

I swallowed. I wanted to be done with this horrible man as quickly as possible, so I pressed on. "Why would Grace try to kill Frank? She knew he was a Pinkerton, but she assumed he was investigating her brother's gambling. Unless—" I broke off at Marsh's nod.

"She knew I was planning to spend time with Frank," he said. "Thursday night was often when we—well…. Anyway, she told me she couldn't meet this week, because it was so close to the wedding and too many people about. I'd said it was all right because the Hamiltons' driver was going to try to pinch some of the good brandy from his master and promised to share it with me."

"She didn't warn you away from him because he was a detective?"

"I don't think she learned that until later. And Bancroft kept me busy with work all day."

I bit my lip as I thought. What would Grace have done if she couldn't warn Marsh about Frank? She would have kept a close eye on one or both of them. Had she eavesdropped on their conversation without Frank picking up on her presence?

"Did you tell Frank about your affair with Grace?" I asked. "And about Eunice confronting you both the night she died?"

Marsh made a face. "It's all a blur. I can't remember."

"I think we must assume Grace either feared that was the case, or knew it for a fact. She took matters into her own hands to protect herself. Just as she did two years ago."

He shuddered. "She's a very determined woman." He slouched forward, head in his hands. "I've made a real mess of things."

No one in the room bothered to dispute that.

Bennett drew me aside and murmured, "I assume we're going to take him to the police now?"

"Yes—but can you handle him yourself? I have to go back to my family and tell them what's going on." Not a conversation I relished. "You'll have to convince the police to visit the Collinsworths and question Grace as soon as possible."

"Once Marsh tells them the whole story," Bennett said grimly, "I don't think it will take much convincing."

"I'll need a hansom—assuming there are any out in this weather."

"I'll make sure of that before I leave." His eyes crinkled with worry. "You're not going to perform any lady-detective heroics while I'm gone, are you? Such as catching the murderer single-handedly before the police arrive?"

"I've done enough of the constabulary's work for them," I said lightly. "One must allow them to earn their pay, after all."

His mustache twitched at that. "Sounds fair enough."

"I'm sorry, miss, we can't go no farther," the cab driver called down.

I stuck my head out to see an enormous oak sprawled across the road. My heart sank. This was the primary route to the mansions along this stretch, which meant the police wouldn't be able to reach the Collinsworth house by vehicle either.

I pulled my hood up. "I'll walk from here, thank you."

He shrugged. "Good luck."

Although it was less than a mile to the Ashton cottage, I was a sodden mess by the time I reached the front drive. To my astonishment, Papa and Reg Collinsworth were hurrying out, clad in rain gear and sturdy boots. The gardener and his boy, carrying ropes and a hook, weren't far behind.

"Pen," Papa said in a breathless voice, "we're joining a group of rescuers at the shore. A fishing boat has foundered in the storm." He touched my arm. "Stay here with the ladies— Miss Collinsworth is here as well. She came to apologize, apparently—and in such weather! Your mother is thawing some-what." He dropped his voice. "When I get back, you can tell me what happened at Bancroft's."

There was quite a lot to tell, but I could only get my mind around one thing at the moment. Grace Collinsworth was *here*. What was her real reason? Not to apologize, certainly. No—she wanted to find out more about Frank's condition, and if she was at risk of being exposed.

"Be careful, Papa," I called absently to his departing back.

Reg Collinsworth lingered, however. The rain dripped off his nose as he stood, shifting from one foot to the other. "Miss Hamilton, I wish to…to apologize to you."

"Apologize?"

"After I intercepted your note from Shaw the other day, I told Reeves about it. I'm sorry to say we had a joke at your expense about you having some sort of assignation with a strange man. And now it turns out that Reeves was…I mean…." His voice trailed off as he looked down at his boots, the water dripping from the top of his hood.

"Has Officer Jance turned up evidence that Reeves murdered Shaw?" I asked.

"He found Reeves' dinner jacket—the cuff was bloodstained —along with the mate to the onyx cufflink left in the barn. Jance brought me the cufflink to identify."

"They were yours, I take it? And Reeves had borrowed them from you?" There'd been no time to search through Collinsworth's jewelry as I'd planned. Once I was confident of Reeves' guilt, it had seemed plausible that Reeves helped himself to Collinsworth's cufflinks. He'd had no compunction at taking other things—the cigars, for example.

"No," Collinsworth said. "I'd given him a set just like mine several days ago because he'd admired them so." He shook his head, sending water rivulets off the brim. "He's been so jealous and bitter toward me lately. I thought it would appease him."

I stiffened. "You've appeased him all too often, Mr.

Collinsworth—abasing yourself to his petty level, time and again. Sharing my private communication with him was merely the latest instance."

Collinsworth's voice was subdued and I strained to hear it over the wind that tore at my hood. "It seemed a harmless bit of gossip. I had no idea it would have such dreadful consequences."

"Dreadful indeed," I snapped, too cold and too wet to mince words. I drew breath to tell him about his sister, but the words died on my lips as I watched him digging his booted toe into the mud, not even able to meet my eye. He looked so miserable. I hadn't the heart to do it.

"Reg!" Papa had returned up the path. "Come along, we're waiting for you!"

Collinsworth flashed me an anguished look before turning away.

I stepped onto the porch, teeth chattering, and hesitated with my hand at the door. There was no hurry to join the ladies in the parlor—no one was expecting me. Far preferable to face a murderess while wearing dry clothes, I reasoned. In fact, Pinkerton would be wise to add that tip to his operatives' guide.

I went around to the kitchen door. My growling stomach reminded me that I'd missed luncheon.

Mrs. Mullins was drying the last of the dishes and passing them to a girl to put away. She let out a squeak.

"Sorry to startle you," I said.

The woman clucked her tongue as I dripped upon her clean floor. "Land sakes, Miss Hamilton, I canna believe you've been out in this awful storm."

I gratefully accepted my second towel of the day. "It really is something out there. The driver had to drop me off a mile back. A tree came down."

"Lotsa trees are coming down, by the sound of it," the cook said darkly. "Don't know how folks'll be traveling for the wedding tomorrow. The roads'll be a mess for days. Trains are sure to be delayed, too."

"Has there been talk of postponing the ceremony?" I asked.

Mrs. Mullins shrugged. "Nobody tells me anything. All I know is the day staff is gonna be sleeping here tonight."

"A wise precaution." I handed back the damp towel. "I'd better go change and find out what's going on."

"Ya want somethin' to eat first?"

As it also seemed wise to face a murderess on a full stomach, I gratefully accepted the offer.

I finished my soup and buttered roll and hurried upstairs. Once I had on dry clothes I pulled out the bottom bureau drawer and felt underneath for my lockpicks and derringer.

The gun was gone.

CHAPTER 24

*J*paced the confines of the bedroom. No one but
Cassie knew my hiding place. I couldn't think of a
single reason why she would take my derringer. And wouldn't
she have left a note to explain? She knew I'd be alarmed to find
it missing.

Who else in the house would have known I had a gun to
steal? Only my parents and Bridget knew I was a detective,
unless someone else had figured it out.

Someone who already knew Frank was a detective.

Shaking my head and feeling distinctly vulnerable, I went
downstairs. Before joining the ladies in the parlor, however, I
made a detour to Lord Ashton's gun room.

I spied just what I was looking for, in a display case mounted
over the mantel—a pair of lovingly restored Colt Single-Action
Army revolvers. The barrel was cavalry-length, so it was a bit on
the long side for me, but it looked to be my best option. One of
them would do.

The case was locked, drat it. I should have expected that—
these were collector's showpieces. Did I have time to go back up
to the bedroom for my lockpicks?

I bit my lip. Word of my arrival in the kitchen would have been widely broadcast by now. I'd be missed soon enough.

I surveyed the room and turned toward a tall cabinet—this one unlocked, mercifully—that contained short-barrel hunting rifles. I took one down from its hook and hefted it. Heavy, but manageable. I'd used something similar on hunting trips with Papa, though that was ages ago. I found the ammunition, loaded it, then held it down along my skirts as I turned down the main corridor toward the parlor. I couldn't very well walk in with a loaded shotgun—but where to set it aside if needed?

In the hall just outside the parlor door I spotted a tall, decorative vase sporting a tufted seagrass arrangement. I carefully lowered the rifle, barrel first, in among the stems and rearranged them to conceal it.

I don't know why, but now I felt better. I smoothed my skirts, took a breath, and walked in.

The parlor had a vigorous fire going, a tray of tea and comestibles lay at Bridget's elbow, and the drapes were closed against the ravages of the storm outside. All quite cozy.

Mother looked up as I entered. "Ah, Penelope. We were wondering what kept you." She waved me into a chair as I greeted Bridget and Grace, seated together on the divan. Grace looked up with a smile that didn't quite reach her weary eyes. No surprise that she hadn't been sleeping well lately.

"Where are Cassie and Miss Blakely?" I asked.

Bridget poured me a cup of tea and passed it over. "They went to the police station hours ago. Rebecca was exceedingly distressed about Mr. Trent's arrest when Reg came over with the news. She insisted upon going to see him."

Ah, so he'd been arrested, after all.

Mother sniffed. "Most inappropriate. A young lady does not chase down a man who's no better than a common criminal."

Or chase down a man of any kind, I was tempted to add, but decided against it.

"Rebecca would not be deterred, no matter how much we

tried," Bridget went on smoothly—she was obviously accustomed to maneuvering around Mother's criticisms, "so Cassie agreed to go with her. To keep her unladylike impulses in check." Her lips curved as she took a sip from her cup.

"As they haven't returned," Mother said, "we have to assume they're waiting out the storm."

Grace gave a deprecating laugh. "I must admit I'm in a similar situation, imposing upon your kindness to remain here for a while."

Mother's placid expression gave away little. "You are of course welcome to stay as long as you like, Grace."

"Even after the storm, travel by road will be a challenge," I observed. "There's a large oak blocking the main road out of the neighborhood. I had to walk the rest of the way here. No doubt other trees have come down."

"The guests may not be able to travel," Bridget said.

Mother got up, went to the window, and pulled the curtain aside. "The roses are no doubt ruined, too. The gardener's boy didn't have the prudence to snip them ahead of time."

"You told him to wait until late in the day, as I recall," I reminded her.

I ignored her glare and turned to Bridget. "What are you going to do?"

"I don't know. Reg and I will have to discuss it when he returns."

I glanced over at Grace. A shawl was bunched in her lap as if she were cold, and she sat stiffly, her gaze flicking to Mother and me.

The conversation subsided into an awkward silence, punctuated only by the crackling fire and the sounds of rain and wind buffeting the windows. We all seemed to be at a loss for polite, innocuous topics.

I knew why I felt tongue-tied, of course. I'd been in the presence of murderers before, but never before had it been necessary to maintain a pretense of ignorance.

If we were to get through this until the police arrived, I had to stiffen my resolve and set aside the image of Frank in a hospital bed, bandaged and unconscious.

I inclined my head toward Grace. "Papa said you came out in such weather to apologize." I gestured at Mother. "I hope this means that all is mended?"

"Of course," Mother said.

Her clipped tone fooled no one. Grace quivered with indignation. "I'm sure you can understand the shock of learning a detective has been looking into one's private affairs. At the behest of the bride's family, no less."

Bridget flushed. "Not at my behest, Grace."

Grace patted her hand in a conciliatory gesture. "No one is blaming *you*, my dear." She turned to my mother. "You had only to ask, Mrs. Hamilton. We have nothing to hide. I hope Reg made that clear to your husband last night. Is there anything else you wish to know?"

Mother's nostrils flared briefly as she turned my way. "How is Mr. Wynch, Penelope?"

I blinked in surprise. She despised the man, but I welcomed the change of topic.

Grace sat up straighter in her chair. "Ah, yes—I'd heard about that. It's a wonder he survived."

I kept my eyes on my mother, not trusting my facial expression at the moment. "He's still unconscious."

"Your father tells me," Mother said, "that you were going to Rosecliff to speak with Mr. Bancroft's secretary—a fellow named March, is it?—about Frank's accident."

Out of the corner of my eye I saw Grace go rigid.

Oh-ho, the cat was out of the bag now. Perhaps there wasn't cause for worry—where could Grace go, after all, even if the police were delayed?

Still, my missing derringer made me uneasy. How she'd managed it I didn't know, but I was convinced she had it. The bunched shawl in her lap…I dearly hoped the rifle could stay in the vase, unused. "Yes, I did go to Bancroft's to speak to the secretary. His name is Marsh."

Bridget looked up in interest. Here finally was a conversation about something other than weather or wedding plans. "Oh? Why was that?"

"He was the last known person to see Fra—Mr. Wynch—last night."

Mother narrowed her eyes. "You're sure of this?"

I nodded. "Except for his attacker, of course."

"Attacker?" Bridget asked. "It wasn't an accident?"

"It was deliberate. It's quite similar to Eunice Collinsworth's supposed accident."

Mother perked up at that. She narrowed her eyes thoughtfully at Grace. That lady was silent, her face expressionless.

Bridget frowned in confusion, glancing between us. Finally, she gave up and asked, "What did Marsh have to say?"

"He wasn't there. Mr. Bennett and I intercepted him at the train station, however. He was trying to flee."

Grace expelled a quiet sigh and sat back against the cushions. "Ah, the guilty ones always do. I take it Marsh was responsible for what happened to Mr. Wynch? He would deny it, of course."

"He does deny it," I said, "though I grant you he would be the obvious suspect. He claims he was too intoxicated to even walk home under his own power last night and that Mr. Wynch had to help him."

"That explains why Wynch was found so close to Rosecliff," Mother murmured, half to herself. "But why would Marsh flee if he isn't guilty?"

Bridget leaned forward, intrigued by the puzzle. "Perhaps he knows who did it. He's afraid."

Smart girl.

But one glance at Grace's hands, gripped within the folds of the shawl in her lap, was enough to make me hesitate to reveal any more. The woman's nerves were strained to the breaking point. Better to wait for the police.

I stood. "If you'll excuse me, I believe I'll read in the library. This morning's experience has been fatiguing." I could keep an eye on the front door from there, in case Grace decided to leave in spite of the storm.

"Oh, no you don't," Bridget protested. "You can't leave us hanging like that. You said you caught up to him. What did he tell you?"

"Not much. Mr. Bennett took him to the police. The matter is now in their hands."

Mother's frown had cleared, and she once again turned her sharp eyes and hawkish nose upon Grace.

I knew that look all too well. Mother had figured out the reason for my evasions.

I tried to head off the confrontation that was bound to follow. "Mother," I began, "if you would step out to the corridor, there's something I want to"—

"It is *you* who is responsible, is it not?" Mother demanded, her tone as imperious as any blueblood matron can achieve. "*You* tried to kill Frank Wynch. Why? Were you protecting your brother yet again? Did he kill his first wife after all?"

Bridget emitted a stifled shriek.

"No, Mother," I said calmly. "Reg didn't do it. Grace killed Eunice."

Bridget caught her heel in her hem as she tried to scramble up from her seat and away from Grace. When I stepped over to help her, Grace reached under her shawl and drew out my derringer. She grabbed Bridget around the upper arm, stood, and yanked the sobbing girl upright.

"Grace! Put the gun down," I said.

Instead, she gave me a frantic look and started dragging Bridget to the door.

I followed her, step by step, as she retreated with Bridget. I could feel Mother moving as well. "Let her go, Grace. This will gain you nothing."

"We were *fine*," Grace spat, "until the all-mighty Hamiltons had to interfere."

"Where do you hope to go? You know you can't get away." I inched closer.

Grace gave me a contemptuous glare. "You thought you were so clever, didn't you? But I knew something was amiss. When I learned that man was a detective, I realized you two seemed awfully close—holding hands, exchanging private glances. That's when I knew you must be working together."

"So you searched my room," I said calmly. Better to keep her talking.

"It was easy to make an excuse and slip in there," she gloated. "It didn't take that long to find *this*." She adjusted her grip on the derringer.

I obviously needed a better hiding place in the future.

I took another step.

"No!" She shifted the gun to where Mother stood. I looked over my shoulder to see my mother's hand reaching toward the bell pull beside the hearth.

It was a good try, but a maid hurrying in to face a gun-wielding, unstable female was the last thing we needed right now.

Mother froze.

"Apparently I need to keep my eye on the both of you," Grace said. "Therefore, Miss Hamilton, you and your mother will precede us out into the hall."

I went over to Mother and looped my arm through hers. I could feel her tremble in my grip. "We'll do as she says," I murmured. "It will be all right."

Grace watched us, carefully stepping back with Bridget as we approached the doorway. I was glad to see my cousin had recovered her composure. Her eyes were steady as they met mine. She was waiting for an opportunity.

As tempted as I was to give her one, Grace was watching me carefully. A sudden lunge to disarm her was too risky. I needed an unguarded moment.

I kept Mother close, stepping ahead of her slightly in an attempt to block Grace's view of where my hand was going next, once I was through the door. The vase.

Mother's eyes widened as she spotted the shotgun in its ludicrous hiding place, but she quickly smoothed her face to an expressionless mask and pivoted sideways to better block Grace's view. Even under trying circumstances, my mother, bless her, is a quick-witted woman.

Grace was close behind us—too close. I stood in front of the vase and waited for her to pass, praying she wouldn't glimpse the shotgun. Thankfully, she was too busy keeping her grip on the derringer in one hand and Bridget's arm in the other. "One of you," she ordered, "move ahead of us and open the front door."

And what then?" I asked in exasperation.

"That's my business. You don't think I came here without a plan, once I learned Wynch had survived?" Her voice turned steely. "Quickly, now."

"I'll do it," Mother said, with a meaningful look at me. I'd brought the shotgun. By her reasoning, it was only fair that I got to wave it around.

Grace turned her head briefly to watch Mother's progress, which gave me the moment I needed. I yanked the gun out of the vase, which teetered and smashed, pulled back the bolt, and leveled the barrel.

Her eyes widened.

"Drop the gun," I said grimly.

She swallowed. "You wouldn't dare shoot me."

Mother had opened the door and returned. She raised an eyebrow my way—in query, or appreciation?—and wisely moved clear of my sight line.

I adjusted the butt more comfortably upon my shoulder.

"Don't count on it. I have shot grouse in Scotland and quail in Kentucky. I'm perfectly capable of using this."

"Oh, I can attest to that," Mother chimed in dryly. "She can drop two guinea fowl in a single shot. I'd take her seriously if I were you."

Bridget, no doubt sensing her captor's hesitation, brought down her boot heel sharply on that lady's arch and twisted out of her grip. The derringer dropped with a clatter.

Bridget had just picked it up when several dripping men burst through the door. The first was Gordon Bennett. He froze at the perplexing tableau of four women—two of them holding weapons—gathered in the middle of the hall.

He met my eye. "The cavalry's here, Miss Hamilton." His lips quirked. "Not that you seem in need of it."

EPILOGUE

Boston, Massachusetts
Friday, July 8, 1887

"*W*ell, that's the last of it," Cassie said, snapping her trunk lid closed and sinking wearily into my mother's favorite mauve wingback chair.

"Did you remember to pack the coffee tin?" I teased.

She made a face at me. "It *is* the perfect size for a cutting."

And an interesting memento. I'd never look at a tin of *Mrs. Acker's Morning Blend Coffee* in quite the same way.

"I'm glad we could stay on long enough to see Bridget and Reg finally married," she went on, "but it's good to be heading home at last."

"I echo that sentiment." I tucked one more skirt into my own case before shutting it. The upheaval and ensuing scandal of Grace's arrest naturally meant the elaborate Newport society wedding had to be canceled. In the end, Bridget and Reg opted for a private ceremony here at my parents' Boston townhome. It took place just the other day, attended by Mother, Papa, Miss Blakely, Cassie, myself, and—miracle of miracles—Frank.

I smiled. My husband had regained consciousness the day after the storm. Though he was expected to make a full recovery, he was in no condition yet to travel by train back to Chicago. Papa had insisted he stay here in their home in the meantime.

Mother could hardly refuse, of course, as Frank had nearly lost his life in pursuit of the answers she'd sought. But I suspected she'd also begun to thaw toward him. She hadn't dropped a single *that man* reference these past two weeks.

Frank had retained his memory of what happened the night he was injured, and his account of Grace's surprise attack upon him on the dark path after he'd seen Marsh home, coupled with Marsh's own statement about the argument between Grace and Eunice the night the latter had met her end, was more than enough to bring charges against her. Of course, Grace's gun-wielding antics when she tried to escape during the storm only emphasized her dangerous instability. Reg was working even now to convince the authorities that his sister should be confined to a quiet asylum instead of prison.

A brisk knock broke into my thoughts, and the maid poked her head around the partly open door. "Miss Hamilton? A Mr. Bennett has come to call. He wishes to speak with you and Mr. Wynch. Since Mr. Wynch is already settled in the library, I've put the caller in there. Is that acceptable?"

I blinked. "Gordon Bennett is *here?*" I exchanged a puzzled glance with Cassie. "Yes, of course, the library's fine. Tell them I'll be right down."

"Yes, miss." She gave a bob and left.

I glanced in the mirror, smoothed my hair, and re-worked a few pins. "I wonder what he wants."

Cassie frowned. "It's unlikely to be anything good."

. . .

Gordon Bennett stood politely as I entered the library. He was meticulously dressed as usual, the navy, double-breasted jacket fitting smoothly across narrow shoulders and emphasizing his trim build. "Miss Hamilton, how nice to see you again, under more pleasant circumstances."

I inclined my head. "You're looking well, Mr. Bennett. I see you and Mr. Wynch have become acquainted." I nodded toward Frank, who was ensconced upon the sofa, a cushion propping up his injured leg. Though an underlying weariness was still evident in the set of his shoulders, his head wounds were healing and he had a healthy tint to his cheeks.

Frank smiled up at me. "Indeed we have. Come, sit. Gordon was catching me up."

I suppressed a snort as I took a chair. *Gordon?* The two had become quite chummy in such a short time. "What brings you here, Mr. Bennett?"

Bennett crossed his legs and leaned back. "I was surprised to learn Collinsworth and his new bride were back in Newport yesterday. Even more surprising, they're staying at the Ashtons' cottage instead of his own estate. Why is that?"

The newspaper mogul's quick acquisition of new developments never failed to astonish. His adept dodging of questions until he was good and ready to answer them, on the other hand, I was more than familiar with.

I stifled a sigh. We'd get to my question eventually. In the meantime, I was willing to play along. "Reg feels honor-bound to look after his sister, no matter how abhorrent her actions. He's back in Newport to meet with the attorneys and determine what happens next. As Bridget refuses to stay at Gull's Bluff but doesn't want to be apart from him, this was the compromise." Not much of a honeymoon for the beleaguered newlyweds, I thought with a grimace. At least they were together, and the cloud of suspicion over Reg Collinsworth had been lifted at last.

Bennett quirked his light-brown mustache thoughtfully. "Didn't know the fellow had such loyalty in him."

"Bridget saw his better qualities before the rest of us did," I conceded. "So tell us—how is Newport society at large dealing with the back-to-back scandals of the check-forging scheme and Grace's perfidy?"

Out of the corner of my eye I saw Frank stiffen.

"The revelations pertaining to Miss Collinsworth have quite eclipsed the check-forging operation," Bennett said. "It seems the gossip-mongers prefer to fix upon one scandal at a time." His expression turned sheepish. "I cannot deny a selfish sense of relief at that, as it has worked in my favor."

Frank shifted his leg on the ottoman. "What of Shaw's murder? I understand Officer Jance recovered evidence that implicates Reeves."

"Correct. Once Trent recanted his alibi that he and Reeves were together the entire evening, Reeves knew they had him. He finally signed a confession." He flashed me a troubled look. "A *full* confession."

I bit my lip. "I see—so that's why you've come. Reeves told the police about Shaw's note to me, which Reg had related in jest to him. The police now know I was the 'new client' Shaw was to meet the night he was killed."

"A crucial detail for you to withhold," Bennett pointed out dryly.

"I didn't have a choice at the time," I retorted.

"So what happens now?" Frank asked. "Is Pen in trouble with the police?"

Bennett plucked a speck of lint from one impeccably trousered knee. "I had a talk with Jance as soon as I found out. The fellow wasn't as annoyed as you might assume. In fact, he's willing to let it go."

I blinked in surprise. "Really?"

"I suspect he's embarrassed about not catching on to your prevarication," Bennett said, "especially when he knew you'd searched Shaw's room within hours of the body coming to light."

"Well, whatever the reason, I appreciate you interceding on my behalf, Mr. Bennett."

"It was the least I could do." He grinned. "Helping you chase down Marsh and then a murderess in the middle of a thunderstorm was the most fun I've had in years. I live an incredibly dull life compared to you, Miss Hamilton."

I very much doubted that.

He glanced over at Frank. "The *two* of you," he corrected. His gaze flicked to my husband's propped leg. "Although I can see it's not without its hazards."

Frank shrugged. "Could have been worse."

"Well, I must be going." Bennett reached for his hat and stood, as did I. "Is there anything else I can do for you, Miss Hamilton? I am at your disposal."

"There's one thing, if you would. Rumors may be circulating in Newport that I'm a detective. Grace Collinsworth had discovered it. She's likely to tell anyone who'll listen."

He frowned. "Why worry about that?" His eyes crinkled in humor. "Do you plan a return to Newport to uncover more malfeasance, dear lady?"

Frank smothered a chuckle.

I shot him a look before turning back to Bennett. "I'm thinking of my mother. Such talk would subject her to ridicule and undermine her standing among her set. She'd already dealt with Lady Ashton's gossip on the subject, and now"—

"Ah, I see your point," Bennett said. "I doubt anyone will believe the ravings of an adulterous murderess, but I promise to be vigilant. All rumors to that effect will be firmly squelched." He bowed over my hand. "It's been a pleasure. Good-bye, Miss Hamilton."

"Goodbye."

"An agreeable fellow," Frank said, once the door had closed behind him. He leaned his head back and closed his eyes.

I came over to sit beside him. "How are you feeling? Shall I ring for the footman to take you back to bed?"

Eyes still closed, he reached for my hand and clasped it. "Don't bother. I'll be all right."

"You've been rather subdued these past two weeks," I said. "Is something on your mind?"

He looked at me briefly before turning away. "You wouldn't understand."

I frowned. When sober, he was rarely moody like this. "Are you worried you won't fully recover? The doctor is quite confident you will."

He waved a hand in irritation. "This shouldn't have happened in the first place."

"Nonsense, you're a Pinkerton. None of us comes away unscathed in this business. A sniper shot you in the shoulder only two years ago, and back in the old days…remember when Kid Glove Rosie broke a perfume bottle over your head when you caught her shoplifting? A very large bottle, as I recall."

He winced.

Ah. I folded my arms. "Are you telling me you're sulking because a *woman* got the better of you?"

"I am *not* sulking," he muttered.

"Without the rock, the cliff, and the pitch-black night in her favor, I doubt Grace would have succeeded," I teased mildly.

He shot me a look, then grinned. "True enough."

"And we've seen that it takes a lot to kill you," I added.

He sighed. "But if I hadn't been lying in that hospital bed, you wouldn't have needed to defend yourself against her. I could have protected you."

"But I didn't need your protection, did I?"

His gaze was warm and lingering. "I forget sometimes how very capable you are."

I felt my cheeks flush as I waved off the compliment. "Lady Ashton's vase, sadly, did not survive the experience."

He shook his head. "Whatever was Grace thinking, taking Bridget by gunpoint? She couldn't have escaped into the storm."

"Reg and I were talking about that before he and Bridget

left for Newport," I said. "He learned that Grace had made a substantial cash withdrawal and purchased a steamer ticket the morning I found you alive. She was to sail out of the Port of New York to Antwerp the next day. There was a friend of hers who lived there—Count de Claes."

"Then why did she stop at your cottage at all? Why not make her escape directly?"

"I'm speculating here, but I believe she was reluctant to leave her comfortable life unless it was absolutely necessary. Remember, she'd gotten away with murder once before. I imagine she wanted to learn your condition first. If you were likely to awaken, then she'd have to put her plan in place. If not, she would have waited you out."

"A cool customer," he said.

"Until Mother confronted her. Then she panicked. The wiser course would have been for her to simply leave, as if deeply insulted, then quickly proceed with her plan of escape. Instead, she grabbed Bridget."

The mantel clock let out a tinny chime.

"Heavens, it's getting late." I stood. "Cassie and I have to leave for the station in just a few minutes." I held out a hand. "Your help has been invaluable, Frank. Thank you."

He clasped my hand and gently pulled it toward him, kissing the bare place on my inner wrist just above the glove. It's a spot that always makes me shiver. A smile curved his lips. "Take care of yourself, Pen. I'll see you soon. In fact, I have a feeling we'll be seeing more of each other from now on."

If wishes were horses, beggars would ride. I shrugged and withdrew my hand. "Goodbye."

Mother was waiting for me in the front hallway. "Cassie is outside with the coach overseeing the luggage. You've already said goodbye to your father, I trust?"

I nodded. "I want to thank you both for providing for Frank's convalescence. I know that must be difficult for you in particular."

She shrugged. "He's not so very disagreeable."

I turned my chortle into a cough. Mother's roundabout way of expressing grudging respect never failed to amuse me.

She held out an envelope. "I have your payment for the successful conclusion of the inquiry. I hope it's sufficient. I have no experience in such matters."

I did a quick count of the bills inside. "More than enough. Thank you." I passed it back.

Her eyes widened. "You won't accept it?"

"Taking care of Frank while I'm gone is payment enough. But"—I touched the envelope—"there's something I'd like you to do with this. Can you ask Papa to inquire about Johnston Shaw's next of kin? He may have a wife who could use the money. His employer, Gold Star Investigations, can tell you more, I expect."

"Of course." She clasped my hand. "I hope we see you again soon."

My throat tightened. "I would like that."

"Though not to investigate a crime," she added quickly. "Just an ordinary visit."

"Speaking of which," I said, "should rumors about me being a detective circulate among the Newport set, Gordon Bennett has promised to squelch them. I didn't want you to worry."

Her lips twitched as she held the door open for me. "I never thought I'd see the day when the daughter who ran off with a private detective and became one herself would be concerned with society gossip. Perhaps there's hope for you, after all."

She didn't see me roll my eyes as I turned toward the door.

Don't count on it.

THE END

AFTERWORD

I hope you enjoyed the book! Please consider leaving a quick review at your favorite online venue. A single sentence as to whether or not you liked it, along with clicking on the star rating you see fit, can go a long way! Ratings create a digital "word of mouth" that help readers find books they will love, particularly those written by independently published authors. Thank you!

~

DON'T MISS ANY OF K.B.'S RELEASES! SIGN UP AT
KBOWENMYSTERIES.COM/SUBSCRIBE

MYSTERIES SET IN LATE-19TH CENTURY HARTFORD, CT

THE CONCORDIA WELLS MYSTERIES

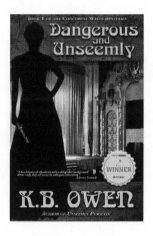

*S*et in a fictitious 1890s women's college, this cozy-style series features Miss Concordia Wells, a young lady professor who cannot resist a little unseemly sleuthing when those she cares about are at risk. Who knew higher education could be...murder?

Start with:

Dangerous and Unseemly, book 1. Winner of **Library Journal's** *"Best Mystery of 2015: SELF-e"!*

"A fun historical whodunit with a delightful background of the early days of women's collegiate education."
~Library Journal

ALSO BY K.B. OWEN

ABOUT THE AUTHOR

K.B. Owen taught college English at universities in Connecticut and Washington, DC and holds a doctorate in 19th century British literature. A long-time mystery lover, she drew upon her teaching experiences in creating her amateur sleuth, Professor Concordia Wells and from there, lady Pinkerton Penelope Hamilton was born.

kbowenmysteries.com
contact@kbowenmysteries.com

Made in the USA
Middletown, DE
10 July 2020